T0146432

FACES
OF
DEATH

FACES OF DEATH

THE URBAN KILLERS OF LEGEND

MONTY

FACES OF DEATH
THE URBAN KILLERS OF LEGEND

iUniverse books may be ordered through booksellers or by contacting:

iUniverse
1663 Liberty Drive
Bloomington, IN 47403
www.iuniverse.com
1-800-Authors (1-800-288-4677)

ISBN: 978-1-5320-5030-5 (sc)
ISBN: 978-1-5320-5031-2 (e)

Print information available on the last page.

iUniverse rev. date: 05/15/2018

Contents

CHAPTER 1

A New Beginning

A start of a new beginning is what Jill & her fellow comrades needed after a hellish nightmare took place exactly five months ago. When they all was caught up in the killers evil twisted plans of revealing the secrets behind who is responsible for the killing that took place this past halloween? However, the finger was still pointed directly toward Jasmine & Thomas who just disappear in thin air. Without any traces of their where'a'bouts? Which so happens to be at the last possible moment when things became critical do to the circumstances. That would eventually sum up the conclusion, as of how their bodies were never discover that night. The fact that Thomas fake his own death that night in the woods near Jill's house. Prior to him being discover as one of the four participant involve in the scuffle later on that night. In a strange twist of events that by coincidence he & Jasmine had on the exact same costume as the others. Which states the obvious on a well thought out plan by manipulating the situation. Which ensued in a conflict between them. As they try to determine who is the killer? Which seems pretty bizarre considering how it all ended that night in the Galleria hall.

Who I might add? Also try to frame Jason as the prime suspect in order to remain undetected. While Jasmine lure them all to the Galleria hall that night claiming that she was held hostage by the killer. Which made all the sense in the world of how it all play out in the end. However, Jill still wasn't convince that the killer is dead & that the two of them are still out there some where's waiting to strike else where? Which wasn't going to be a problem now that the police know who they are? And that they had everything under control. The police made it known throughout the country as they posted Jasmine & Thomas

1

photos all over the national news. Thinking that someone is bound to see one of them, (if not both of them) somewhere's close by.

As it suddenly became clear to the police that the two of them is without a shot of a doubt hiding out some place near the city. As they try to outsmart the police by making them believe that they relocated to another area. Which made the police take extreme measure by putting taps on their love one's. Which instantly turn turmoil as Jasmine & Thomas parents denied there child's involvment in the killing that took place. It seem as if the police didn't care how long it took to solve this case. They wasn't going to stop until they got to the bottom of it. In the meanwhile Jill & the others went there separate ways as time went on. Jill & Jason relationship became an on & off thing that eventually led to them breaking-up for good.

Which led Jill to transfer schools somewhere's out of state which was an excellent move on her part. Considering the problems she had at home involving her parents that went sour. Things just didn't seem right with her parents the day after halloween. Even though, it breaks her heart knowing that she doesn't have a solid relationship with her parents anymore. Then again? She manage to shoulder the load on her own by continuing to move forward with her life. Which is turning out to be the best decision she has ever made. While the same couldn't be said about her ex-boyfriend Jason" who is struggling to make ends meet in a way that has him striving for a better life. His predicament is far way worser than Jill's? As the comparison between the two is unmistakable. After college Jason decided to chase his long term dream of being a local camera man for channel five news. To take part in the quest of finding the truth behind the Faces of death masks in order to bring everything to light.

However, that little dream of his didn't go according to plan as he hope it would. So instead, he decided to take manners into his own hands by conducting his own investigation by going into business himself. Which by the way isn't going so well as he try to come up with a solution that would solve this conspiracy on finding the missing pieces to the puzzle. Not to mention the story Eric lay on them about his involvement in the endless cycle of being a victim in the killer's plot. That had him on the run this entire time as things began to unfold. Which brings up his situation on the fact that he has disappear along with the wind since that night in the school hall. Who I might add is still on the run from the police. Do to the fact that he is still a suspect in this case. The police was still on the hunt in pursuing their killer which was Eric. They believe *that he is responsible for these horrifying events that took place for the last two years. Thinking that he has a major role in all this controversy by fooling the others into believing his heart felt story. As Jill & the others try to explain to the police his side of the story. Thinking that maybe it would get him off the hook.*

Which is kind of difficult to believe when his fingerprints matches the murder weapon. That was use to kill the Hatchet's along with several other teenagers? Which by the way was printed in the morning paper by a certain individual who go by the name of Christian Bell. Who move up from being a school journalist to a columnist for a local newspaper company. To Christian this was nothing more than a part-time job. As his main focus was on attended school full-time in order to achieve his degree of being a full-time journalist. It seem as if Christian is doing well for himself even though he still has nightmares about all that went on at the galleria hall that night. Which causes him to wake up in full sweat doing the middle of the night. "Then again", who wouldn't after all that has went on? However though, it seem as if Christian is still attending the same school. Which isn't smart on his part. Knowing that there's a good chance the killers may still be lurking around the area, according to the police?

Which didn't seem to bother him in the least considering all that went on there. He whether not let it get to him emotionally as a standard problem & wanted to get on with his life. As for the other students that attended Jason's party that night ended up under investigation as the police book them all in for questioning to get the full scoop on what they made have witness or seen that would help them ID the killers. Who is responsible for the killing that took place this past halloween. As evidence show that there is no connection that links the two suspects Jasmine & Thomas to the crime. Which led the police on a wild goose chase. With no evidence provided to the case that would confirm the two is link to the murders. Other than some speculation that says Eric is the prime suspect. It seem as if the police was going around in circle's with no intention on arresting anyone. Do to the fact that they had no leads or traces of any kind that would bring some sort of light to this case that is pending. Then suddenly! it darn on the police that maybe it would be a great idea if they patrol the streets in the neighborhoods around the city this coming halloween.

They made a plan to send out undercover cops to walk the streets at night. Thinking that they may have a better chance of catching the killer in the act this time around? Figuring that they have the solution to this problem & that the situation would be much safer at this year halloween event. The police is very confident that their plan is going to work by spoiling the killer's gameplan of a third reckoning. Considering that the police is kind of underestimating the killers true potential of portraying the brilliance of a great mind. Which would reduce to another brilliant plan that states thee obvious of adapting to new surrounding. Of keeping a low profile until the time present itself once again. By causing all sort of hell on a very special night which includes fear & terror. Which brings up a logical stand point in reference to why the killer is doing all of this? Of what is the real reason behind these killing, "one must ask themselves"?

Figuring that maybe the police could come up with an answer to the million dollar question of why the killers was after Jill & her friends in the first place. Which didn't make no sense what so ever to the police as they try to make sense of it. Taking the time to think this thing over cause some confusion on everyone's mind. Including the police who gave the killers more credit than attended. On why these students & teachers who have no idea what's going on, are made to suffer the killers wrath. Perhaps it could be something personal like a grudge. Which seems more likely to be the case? Who knows what the motives are behind these killings, but whatever it is? Jill & the others wasn't going to stop until they got to the bottom of it. As they all denied having a vendetta with anyone as far as they know. They all just wanted to put this incident behind them & move on with their lives. Which is kind of hard to do when the pressure is on them all of trying to remain under the radar to keep reporters away.

Only to remain hidden from the killers who is still probably out searching for them. Words alone couldn't describe how ironic this nightmare of a story became? As reporters cover the entire incident by getting interviews from local residents. You couldn't imagine the stories that was being told around the country. As this horrifying event would go down. As one of the most horrifying tales that has ever displayed throughout history. However, Jill & the others remain in the clear from the press until this case reach it's verdict.

CHAPTER 2

Old Habbit's Die Hard

Not for one second did Jill forget about the past as it tomented her constantly for the longest. Unable to escape from it's horrifying grib that has taken it's toll on her mentally as a reminder that she can't block out the images that is constantly displaying over inside of her head. Which eventually led to the nightmares she's been having every night for the past three months. However, it didn't stop her progress of maintaining her composer throughout the hard times. Of having to deal with stress a lot of times when she feels depress about certain things that is bothering her. "Like for instant"? Being able to trust certain people, is one of Jill's main issues. Feeling as if there are eyes watching her every move, which makes her feel uncomfortable. Through it all, Jill manage to make some new friends at her new school. Who has help her cope with all of her problems. She manage two new friends who go by names of Amanda Berkeley & Deshawn Williams. They all were sort of like family in a way, as Jill accepted them both as her equal.

They did just about everything together as a group no matter what the circumstances was? Amanda & Jill were roommates as the two of them hit it off from the moment they met & since Amanda was friends with Deshawn. It was only a matter of time before Jill became friends with Deshawn as well. Amanda was sort of on the quiet side you know the type that stood to herself most of the time before meeting Jill. Amanda was kind of in the same predicament Jill was in, about being able to trust people. Do to the fact that she has been tease & pick on constantly by other students just because she's different from the rest. They do it just because they know that they could get over on her. Without her saying a thing about it. Thinking that they can push her around when ever they

5

feel like it. On the other hand it was quite thee opposite for Deshawn who I might add is a practical joker who loves a great prank every now & then? He wasn't the most belove person in the school do to his immature behavior that got him kick out of class a few times.

Many of the other students couldn't stand Deshawn for what he stood for? Do to the fact that you couldn't take him seriously? Deshawn was sort of a jock who took part in different sporting events. That made his teammates look up to him as a leader of some sort, even to some females who took to him as well. It seem as if Deshawn wasn't the most popular student in the school. "Then again"? He wasn't the most hated person in the school either? Which kind of places him somewhere's near the middle of popularity. Which brought his attention to Amanda who he quickly took too. Considering how she reminds him of how he use to be. The two of them became the best of friends when Deshawn stood up for her when no one else would. He even went as far as playing cruel pranks on the people who mistreated Amanda as a way of getting back at them. He did it, out of love to defend her rights as a person just as a big brother would when defending his little sister. And for that? She was deeply in his graces. The two of them became pal's every since then & remain close even to this day. Jill seen the respect the two had for one another & decided that she wanted to be apart of the team. Just as things were beginning to become normal again, in came a surprise of a life time.

When Jill receive an unfamiliar package that was sent from a certain someone who name didn't appear on the box. Jill figure that the package was from a secret admirer. As she starts to read the note that was attach to the package. While opening up the box to see what's inside that is so important that someone wanted her to see. Which place her in a very peculiar position once she look inside & seen the ghost face mask from the movie scream. "Her expression suddenly change"? As fear started to seek into her body once she seen what the note said? Which was the question that agonize her mind with fear. By bringing up the subject on what is her favorite scary movie of all times. Total fear had begun to take it's effect upon her, as she just lost it completely. Jill drop the box & quickly ran out of the room screaming. The intensity was at it's most critical point for Jill. As she started to pay close attention to her surrounding. Thinking that the killers is somewhere's on campus watching her closely. Jill was so out of it? That she didn't notices Amanda & Deshawn standing outside of her dorm room waiting for the results of their little joke to transpire.

Which kind of backfire in their faces on the fact that they went a little too far this time. So the two of them decided to go after her before she get to the campus security. Once they finally caught up with her. Deshawn & Amanda broke the news to her as gentle as they possibly could. Jill became furious at the two of them, do to the fact that they knew her situation. After all she's been through this past halloween of trying to move on with her life. Only for them to pull a stunt such as this to upset her. Despite the fact that she knew what kind of person Deshawn was, but as far as "Amanda goes"? Jill thought that she would be the last person in the world to do this sort of thing to her. Being that they were friends & all? Based on the fact that they understood one another. Which goes to show her that looks can be deceiving. As it turns out that she was wrong about the both of them & decided to part ways from them. Jill felt embarrass, as she slowly walk back to her dorm room with her head down. Almost feeling as if she has been made a fool of by her two friends.

Deshawn couldn't help, but to feel bad about what he has done to Jill. Giving the fact that it was his idea in the first place to begin with. Amanda was also down in the dumps for her participation in the prank. Knowing that she may have ruin a perfectly good relationship with Jill. Even though, she wasn't really up for it in the first place. Knowing the consequences that may result to something bad happening? Considering that nothing good can come from this sort of action? Thinking that this is the sort of therapy Jill needed. In order to get her to relax a little bit. By showing her the humor side of it, since she is so tense all the time. Come to find out that they both was wrong & that they should've been more understanding. Jill felt betrayed by the people she trusted the most. As she discover who her real friends were. You couldn't imagine Jill's shame as people in the hallways made fun of her. She must have felt helpless & ashamed, considering what she has been through these past couple of months. Prior to last year halloween massacre that sent shock waves across the country of all the merciless killings that took place.

Amanda & Deshawn felt awful about what they done & wanted to know how they can make it up to her. The first thing that they must do is apologize to Jill for what they have done. As it turns out that Jill forgave them both for their foolish behavior. However, she didn't forget what they did? As a reminder to keep a close eye on them from now on. Although, Jill still had her doubt's of uncertainty about the two of them. Feeling that there is more to the story then what they are letting on. That maybe the two of them are hiding something in particular that has Jill concern. It was from that day on, that Jill decided to keep her distance until she can figure out what's going on with the two of them. Which is kind of strange if you think about it? Do to certain details of why Deshawn loves pranking people in particular. Perhaps, it could be a habbit of his? Of trying to make others feel the way he felt when people made fun of him. Maybe, that why he can relate to Amanda? Which is probably why she is so soft spoken? That whatever the reason was for pulling this sort of stunt on her had to be for a certain cause. Otherwise they wouldn't have done it.

That all boils down to the conclusion that no one is that damn quiet not to stand up for themselves when they are wrong. Unless, Amanda has other ways of dealing with certain issues. Which brings up Deshawn on the subject of how he is always there to defend her no matter what the situation is? Then Jill realize something about Amanda that suddenly caught her attention. Involving her & Deshawn little strategy of playing the role of the victims. While you may think that Amanda is so innocent that she wouldn't hurt a fly, but Jill knew better? As it turns out that they both are in on the jokes by playing the hand that was dealt to them. "For instatnt"? If Amanda had a problem with someone in particular, she would simply go straight to Deshawn to give him the heads up that there is a problem that needs to be taking care of? Which has Jill puzzle on whether or not she may have offend Amanda in some way. That would have her to sink to this level, in order to get her point across.

They both didn't have the slightest clue that Jill was on to them & that she couldn't come up with any wrong doing to Amanda except be her friend. She just knew that something wasn't right with the two of them. As Jill try to place her finger on the matter. Then it dawn on her of why they did what they did? Considering the many ways of humoring themselves by playing this sort of joke on April fools day. Which didn't set well with her in the least bit. Meanwhile, Jill couldn't help but to think about her other two friends. Jason & Christian who she hasn't talk too for months. That would soon change when Jill receive an e-mail from her ex-boyfriend Jason saying that he miss her & how he wanted to see her again. He then applied? That the three of them should get together for old times sake at his parents cabin out in the woods by the lake. Where they can have some peace & quiet to reminisce on the good times they share. Jill was uncertain about the whole getting together thing & wanted to know the reason for this outing. Then on top of that? He wanted to schedule the trip two days before halloween which didn't sit well with Jill. "Jason then replied",? That this would be a great way to over come the nightmares. According to his therapist who suggested that he come to terms with this issue. So he can get on with his life. Instead of running from it, which could haunt him for the rest of his life.

If he doesn't break the cycle now! That the reason for this reunion is to reconnect with one another as it should be? Considering that one incident shouldn't break them apart. Of how great things use to be before all the bad stuff starting happening. That the killers wouldn't dare come after them, do to the fact that the police are fully prepare this time around. Jill was still unsure about the get together & needed a friendly advice on what she should do. So she turn to her roommate Amanda & ask, her opinion? Amanda told her that she should go with her feeling & surprise them by showing up. That in fact, it would be a perfect idea if her & Deshawn went along for the ride to keep her company. So that Jill can be at ease while on the road. Which is a splendid idea as Jill accepted Jason's offer on taking the next step. In their process of recovering from tragedy that has impacted their lives. By overcoming adversity with the support of one another.

CHAPTER 3

The Next Step

As time past, Jason decided to gather his equipment so that he & his buddies can film the reunion. Jason thought that maybe it would be some help if they talk about the nightmare that has affected them all emotionally. To try & see if he can break this thing down piece by piece in order to solve the jig-saw puzzle that relates to the faces of death masks. To bring some sort of light to this whole ordeal by stating the facts. He just knew that something was missing in this case of how it all play out in the end. That there were some key elements that was overlook that night in the galleria hall. Feeling as if there is more to the story then the killers had plan. As far as Jasmine & Thomas go's? He just needed everyone's insight on what they witness that night. In order to uncover the true behind Jasmine & Thomas involvment in this case. Jason just knew that he & his two buddies Alan & Jerry could break open this case without even breaking a sweat. The reason Jason seem so cocky is because he knew that Alan was a hounddog who can track a needle in a haystack do to his intelligent brilliant mind. Considering the fact that he is a genius when it comes to this sort of thing.

While on the other hand Jerry comes as an expert in the mystery field of solving anything that is complicated. Do to the fact that he loves to take on a story of this magnitude. Jason was determined to get to the bottom of this story for two reasons. For one? It would increase his chances of becoming a camera man for the channel five news. The most watch news in the city, & as for the second reason. To put an end to this thing once & for all. So that everyone can go on with their lives? Which brings up Eric on the matter of how Jason wanted him to be there with the three of them. So the four of them could resolve the *issue with the three masks. Which seems to be the source to the murders? Eric however, was a non-factor, do to the fact that he is consider as a ghost at this point & time. As he stood hidden away, until the time was right to show his face again. No one really knew Eric's where"a"bouts at the time. Considering that he is wanted for murder by the police who has a five thousand dollar reward out for his capture. Which places him in a very bad predicament do to the fact that people fear him. Which is one of the reasons why Jason wanted to do this, so that he can clear Eric's name.*

Knowing that he was set-up by the killers for whatever reason plays a huge role on how it all relates back to Eric. Which create's a big question mark on his part. As Jason also knew the feeling of being a victim in the killers plot. Which is something the two of them had in common. Jason was determine to bring justices to the civilization on these ritual killing. By seeking out the truth on who is doing what? With these three mysterious masks. That has Jasmine & Thomas names written all over this investigation. Which seems to be the case at this point & time. For all he knows? Thomas & Jasmine may not be the killers that has terrorize their city for the past two years. That they too could of been victimize by someone in particular who has use them both as a decoy to escape the hall that night. Which creates a real problem if this is a case of mistaken identity. Which is why Jason & his two buddies would have to be on their peas & cues to connect the missing pieces to the story. Meanwhile, on the other end" Christian develop a great relationship with a girl he met online. The two would hit it off very quickly by becoming the best of friends. The two would chat daily for hours on certain issue containing to their relationship.

They both had a lot in common considering that the two has yet to meet one another. Discussing their future together is one of the main priority on setting a date to meet? They both agree to meet at the cabin in the woods for the reunion. It felt as if Christian found the girl of his dreams. That suddenly turn his attention away from all of the distractions that has been surrounding him as of late. The fact that he had a very rough time maintaining his paranoia. By thinking that someone is still after him. Which led him to be very cautious around certain people. That would soon change once he met Abigail the girl he met on a dating site. Christian was very curious to see what she looks like in person. All that he knows about her is what she describe to him over the phone. Which was to give him a little insight on how she looks. Meanwhile, he knew what kind of person she was? Based on her remarkable qualities as a person of moral standards. Christian could almost picture Abigail in his mind as he starts to fantasize about her. He just couldn't wait until the day of the reunion so that they can finally meet one another.

Abigail was excited to have this opportunity of a life time to meet someone of her status. So was Christian who quickly took to her as his soul mate. Christian felt as if he was on top of the world at this point in his life. That nothing could stand in between him & destiny of meeting his one true love. While at the same time reuniting with his two pals Jason & Jill. Which to him is the greatest feeling in the world of bring everyone together for the first time since that fatal night. That the three of them need this outing in order to move forward. Almost, feeling as if they need to come together on this horrifying night. To lift the load that is weighing heavily on their minds. To come to terms of dealing with the horror that has been haunting them all for the past couple of months. That this just might be the therapy they need to bring some sort of closer to this nightmare. As they all agree to participate in the gathering. It was very clear to them all that they are not out of the danger zone yet. That they would have to be extremely care not to let the killers in on their little secret.

Knowing that the two killers still lurks in the shadows, waiting for the right opportunity to strike again. Which bother them the most because they didn't know when or where the killers was going to strike next? Which is the million dollar question on the fact that the killers have some unfinished business to attend to with the three of them. "If that's the case". No one really knew what the case was with the two of them. Except for the fact that they love creating chaos on halloween night for no parent reason. Which didn't set well with the people or the police. Who knew there was a reason for these killing. In which they couldn't place their fingers on? On whether Jasmine & Thomas had something to do with these killing or not. Which led police to believe that this was the work of Eric Johnson. Who could manipulate any situation? In order to disengage himself from the equation? Even if it means framing someone else to take the fall. While he continues on with the rampage that seems to involve the three of them in his evil twisted plans. Which creates confusion on the part of Jason, Jill & Christian who still had concerns about where each of them stand considering the circumstances. As they still question each other on whether or not one of them could be the master mind that is pulling the strings.

Only because of how things play out that night, which has everyone under suspicion on the fact that the killers hasn't been found. It was made clear that night in the Galleria Hall that certain aspects seem a bit unusual. Like how Jason & the killer had on the same exact costume that threw everyone else off? Which seems a bit suspicious, considering how it all went down? Which brings up Jill's situation? Considering how she was capture by the killer that night in the galleria hall? Which brings up the situation with the gun. That was use to resolve the issue between Jason & the killer later on that night. When she accidentally shot Jason? Which again depends on how it was portrayed. Then there's Christian? Who plays as the victim by down playing the conflict between Jason & Jill. As they bicker over which one of them is the killer? Which is the perfect alibi in order to draw the attention away from him. Which brings up a very valid point to each of their cases. Since they all wasn't sure on who it is that is causing all of this controversy between them. Which is the main reason for this gathering so that they could solve this thing once & for all? As it turns out? They just wanted to put things in place so that they could solve the million dollar question on who it is & why they are doing this? However, they still didn't want to leave out the possibility of the two suspects Jasmine & Thomas who plays a huge role in the case. Which can play out in either way considering the circumstances of how things are percevied. Which brings up a good point if the killers are amongst them?

CHAPTER 4

The New Role

Things couldn't be better for Jill as she was selected to attend in the school play as one of the characters in the dramatic hit" The Phantom. Jill was so excited that she got the part that she felt the need to let out a sign of relief. That for once in her life she felt important to a certain extend. Being that she can finally focus her attention else where's other than her distractions in life. Thanks! to her ex-boyfriend's advice on moving along with their lives & not dwelling on the past. Along with the support of her two best friends Deshawn & Amanda. She was all pump up to have this opportunity to try her hand at something different for a change. Getting a new leash on life itself by making a step forward. Doing that time Jill found out that she has a secret admirer who just adore her for how great of a person she is? Which brought her attention to this mystery person. This person begin to shower her with all sorts of gifts. Like a new cellphone & a laptop sort of speech. This person was also a huge fan of the phantom & wanted tickets so that he can see her perform live on stage. Then after the show he can reveal himself to her as one of her biggest fans.

Jill was so excited now that she found someone who is interested in her. "Besides Jason"? She couldn't wait to see who this guy was that has set his sites on her. At first she thought it was Jason who is probably behind this whole charade. Given the fact that he still had feeling for her, but that would soon change. When this mystery of a man deliver a dozen of roses to her with a note attach to it. Saying that, "it's a mystery! Of finding true love that is within her grasp"? A line from her script in the play that made her realize that this person maybe involve in the play as well. Amanda then suggested that maybe she should keep an eye open for any kind of sign from a guy who seem curious

*in the least. As time went on, Jill couldn't take the pressure any longer &
wanted to know who this mystery person was. She kind of had a hunch on who
it might be? Based on how this person acts around her. Jill had her eyes set on
the Director name George Larusso as a possibility. Considering how he always
kid around with her. Which is the least of her problems, as she got the same
reaction from other guys as well. Which create's a real problem of finding the
one who actually likes her. Which led her to believe that this guy wasn't going
to reveal himself until he was good & ready.*

*It was made clear that Jill would have to wait until the night of her play
to discover who this person is? Which is sort of a psychological deal by messing
with her mind a little bit. In the meanwhile, Jill decided to focus all of her
attention on the play with the help of her two friends assistance. Jill could care
less about the jokes that was being play on her by Deshawn who loves to kid
around with her. Being that she is now a professional performer & needs a
good laugh to relieve the stress of performing in front of an large crowd. Do
to the fact that Deshawn was teasing her about certain things about the play.
That she can relate too? On some minor details involving her life. Like how she
has a secret admirer who is crazy about her. Only to be amaze by the mystery
itself of searching for that certain someone. The fact that this person has conceal
himself by staying under the radar. In order to hide his true identity. Just like
the phantom in the story is doing to keep things interesting. By keeping things
secretive until the time is right to reveal himself to her. Doing class, Jill receive
a text message from Amanda to see if she wants to attend a party on campus
tonight. That she just might run into the man of her dreams. Jill was excited
about the idea & agree to meet her & Deshawn there for Eight'O'Clock.*

*Only because she had to go to the library in order to finish up her research
paper that is do tomorrow. That she would be kind of late getting to the party.
While at the library Jill receive an unusual phone call from an unknown
number. The caller begin to play games with her just like before at last year's
halloween massacre. Trying very hard to get inside of her head. Jill just ignore
the caller only because she thought it was Deshawn trying to prank her again
because that's what he do? Come to find out that this was no prank call, as
the caller warn her that this wasn't Deshawn. The caller made it very clear to
Jill that this is serious indeed & begin to play mindgames with her. Until she
got the message that this is for real. Jill emotions suddenly change instantly as
she look around the library to only see that she is all alone in there besides the*

librarian who went to the bathroom. That everyone else left kind of early to go to the party. It is sort of weird how things becomes a factor when fear takes affect? Almost as if everything around you becomes a issue that as Jill on edge. Hearing strange noises coming from the library itself felt kind of eerie as the lights begin to shut off one by one leading up to where she was standing at. Jill try running in order to stay within the boundaries of the lighting before it go's off.

Eventually she came to a dead end of the library as Jill found herself in the dark. She then begin to hear footsteps of someone walking slowly toward where she is hiding. Jill then begins to crawl around the shelves. In order to keep away from the killer who is also creeping around the shelves to see where she is? Just as Jill thought that it was safe to stand up to see who it is following her. She made the attempt to remove a couple of books on the shelf to see who is on the otherside of the room. Words alone doesn't describe the intensity of it all! When in came a hand that suddenly grab a hold to Jill's shoulder from behind! While at the same time on the phone with the killer who yell out "I gotcha"! Jill then let out a horrifying scream as she just lost it completely. Come to find out! That it was only the librarian who grab her to tell her that the library will be closing in a few minutes. As the librarian ask Jill? Why are all of the lights turn off?

As they both heard laugher in the background, as all of the lights starts to turn on. Come to find out, that it was Deshawn & a couple of his buddies playing on the phone. As they couldn't help themselves knowing that Jill is an easy target. Jill was furious at the three of them for pulling this sort of stunt. However, Jill would have the last laugh as the librarian had a joke of her own by calling campus security on them for misusing the library for personal gain.

Which is sort of a mistake on their part knowing that they are now in trouble. Which is sort of good news for Jill as she just smile & wave goodbye to them knowing that they wouldn't be able to attend the party tonight. Hoping that he & his pals learn their lesson that what "go's around, comes around"? Jill then left the the library to join the party with her roommate Amanda. When Jill reach the party she seen that there were a lot of students in attendance. In fact, she even knew a couple of people there that she thought would never participate in this sort of thing. Considering how they are perceived? Which go's to show someone that you can't always judge a book by it's cover. This is the sort of thing Jill & Amanda needed to loosen up a bit about their situation on mixing with the crowd. *The party was a blast as everyone enjoy themselves quite a bit. Even for Jill who thought that she would never attend another party again. Who felt kind of relieve once she got to know people. She even try to locate her mystery man at the party. Which is sort of hard to do when there are different guys hitting on her. However, she still had her eyes set on George who seems quite interested in her. Who was also attending the party. Jill still had her doubts on whether or not he was the one.*

As she try to figure him out on a personal level do to the fact that he is kind of on the shy side. Just as Jill was about to go over & talk to him. She suddenly got distracted for a moment by a streaker running around the party like a moron. It was at that moment she miss her opportunity on seeking out the truth about George who just disappear without a trace. That now she would have to wait for the opportunity to present itself again? Jill & Amanda left the party kind of early do to the fact that they both was kind of wasted. In fact, they was so tore up that they past out in an alley near their dormitory. It seem as if Jill was having a nightmare as she seen the killer standing over her with one of the Faces of Death masks on. Who whisper softly into her ear about her greatest fear of all becoming a reality once again? That soon she will come face to face with fear itself? As the killer left her with these fames words to remember. Which is "What is her favortie scary movie of all times. Which is a reminder to her that she should be careful around certain people not knowing their situation that can easy turn tragic for her. Despite the fact that she is being watch closely by someone in particular?

Jill didn't remember a thing that happen after that? As she awoke from this nightmare to find herself lying in her bed. How she got there? Was a mystery itself as she look over at the curtains & seen the morning sun beaming through the window. Jill then turn around to see if Amanda was in her bed, in which she was, sleeping away. Jill decided to get up do to the fact that she has class in a couple of hours. She still felt kind of under the wheather do to the fact that she has a hangover from last night. As she begun brushing her teeth, all she could think of is the nightmare she had that seem so real at the time. As she wonder how in the world did she manage to make it to her bed with no recollection on what happened. As Jill was getting ready for school she had gotten a phone call from Deshawn who explain the situation to her about how they had to help Amanda & her up to their rooms before they get caught by security who was patrolling the area at the time. Which explains everything so far, but what about the dream she had that weigh heavily on her mind. About what she encounter last night, which had her debating on whether she was dreaming or not? The fact that it all felt real to her. The problem is that she was so wasted that she couldn't tell the differents. Which is kind of mind boggling in a way that has her focusing on certain details that was brought up. As Jill remember every detail that was mention to her by the killer, as a reminder. That she can't escape the past under no circumstance. As that part remains a factor in her mind, which is one of her many concerns.

CHAPTER 5

Preparing For Break

Whether it was a dream or not Jill decided to not let it rain on her parade. As she focus all of her attention on the play that is days away. Denying herself that this can't be happening again. That it was all in her mind? That there is no way the killers could of found her. The fact that she is under so much pressure that it is starting to catch up with her. Jill then decided to put her mind at easy so that it wouldn't interfere with her performances. Jill rehearse day in & day out with the cast in order to have perfection & chemistry on set. Everything was going according to plan as it should. As Jill & George relationship begin to build very quickly by the day. They then became the best of friends as he help her become a natural on stage. It didn't matter to her if he was the one or not. She begun to fall for him very hard the more time they spent with one another? Then came the special night for Jill as she look forward to the play & meeting a certain someone. Who promise to reveal himself before the night is over.

Considering everything that happened so far has led to this special moment in time. To finally seek out her mystery man & put an end to all this secrecy. Which didn't matter to Jill as she already knew who this mystery guy was? As she seen George on his cellphone texting away. She then receive a message on her phone shortly afterwards. From her supposedly secret admirer claiming that he will be on the look out for a picture perfect perfomances by her. As the stage was set & ready to bring about some great entertainment to the audience. As this was the moment of truth for Jill to be in the spot light performing in front of a live audience. However, doing the middle of her scene Jill had gotten a unexpected disruption from what seems to be the killer standing up in the rafters. Wearing one of the Faces of Death masks staring down at her the moment the ceiling lights flash in that area. It was sort of a spur of the moment kind of thing as Jill had to take a second glance to see if the killer was actually there.

To her surprise it was nothing to worry about, thinking that maybe she is over worked from not getting enough rest. That maybe she is hallucinating about things that isn't really there. Thinking that maybe her mind is playing tricks on her do to the fact that she is still hung up on the past. As she decided to not let it interfere with her performance. Thinking to herself that the show must go on? She finish the play with an outstanding performance. Letting her work speech for itself by getting a standing ovation from the audience. Jill couldn't believe the reaction she was getting from the crowd. As of how smoothly the performance went. Regardless of what she may have seen in the rafters. Which was a distance memory as Jill turn her attention toward something more promising. Like meeting her mystery man, now that the show is over. She then receive a text on her phone from George, asking? If she understood the point he was trying to make about taking chances in life. That there is no greater feeling than expecting the unexpected to happened. Mainly because of her performance tonight that had a impact on the audience. That there wasn't anyone else who could of done it better.

That there is no other way to express his feelings for her then to let her know personally. From that stand point? Jill finally reveal who her mystery man is? As it all when down the way he said it would. Which wasn't no big surprise for Jill as she kind of knew who he was all along. With that out of the way Jill can now plan their trip to the cabin to meet with the others. Amanda thought that it would be a excellent idea if she invites her new man to the reunion. In which she did, but George turn down the offer do to the fact that he had other plans. As time went on? Jill, Jason & Christian started to chat with one another about life itself. Mainly to keep each other posted on how well they are doing? Jason on the other hand had a very rough time maintaining his lies. Only because he didn't want to feel left out by Jill & Christian's achievements. Jason just wanted to fit in as a equal so he made up all these lies about being a camera man for channel five news. Knowing that he would have to carry out these lies in order to fool the others. By having to wear a fake uniform to convince everyone that he is a camera man for the channel five news with the logo to verify it.

After all, it is going to be halloween when they meet at the cabin. In *which they wouldn't know the difference any way just as the saying go's "no harm, no foul" right! They all just wanted to have a nice quiet weekend to relax & catch up on things. With that said? They all begin to plan out their weekend for this special occasion by giving each other ideas on what they should do? While at the cabin? Instead of reminiscing about last year's halloween massacre. There should be some activities in mind so that they won't be bore to death with nothing to do on this trip. The plan was to have a halloween party of their own to accept the fact that nothing is as bad as it seems. By celebrate this event as a way of getting over the past. Which is going to be amongst the eight of them, as a private party. Which wouldn't involve costumes or masks as the three of them agree to ban it from the camp site. Knowing their friends, however, is a different story when it comes to halloween of obeying the rules that Jason has set. Of trying not to condone this sort of behavior at the party. Which is a understatement? That there was no way their friends are going to abide by those rules? Especially Deshawn, for that matter who loves pranking people.*

Moving along as time starts to past, drawing closer to the reunion. That there are so many surprises just waiting to be reveal at the reunion. Thinking of all the stuff that is going to break news when they all reconnect with one another again? Of all the stories that will be told & recollected about the good & the bad. That this reunion will be one for the ages that they all wouldn't soon forget. Finally the day came to prepare for the road trip. As Jill & her two friends pack the van & got off to an early start on the way to Jason's father cabin. They couldn't imagine how great a road trip can be with all of the sites & adventure that is headed their way. That there is no greater feeling than the three of them on a open road that leads to excitement to feel free to do whatever they want. Which can be said, the same about Christian who also got off to an earl start to finally have the opportunity to meet his mystery woman. Christian just knew that he was in for a surprise when he gets to the cabin. He then sent her a message from his cellphone, asking? If she has already hit the road. "She then reply" by senting him a smiley face to insure him that she is on her way.

As for Jason & his two buddies they arrive at the cabin kind of early to get things straight before the others show up. However, when Jason got out of the car he seen that things was different according to how it use to be? Like how there was two family size cabins side by side from one another near his father's cabin. Which was kind of surprising? Which wasn't part of the conversation between him & his father the night before. The fact that his father didn't mention the two cabin's to him at all. Considering the fact that his father had no idea that it was there in the first place. As Jason gave his father the benefit of the doubt. The three of them decided to past by the joint to get a better look. Alan suggested that maybe they should get the camera's in order to film this as part of the show. Which was a splendid idea as Jason gave the story on these two mystery cabins. Do to the fact that they had no idea who own it? He try to enter the door of the cabin, but it was lock. So instead he look inside the windows & gave a brief statement on how it look from the inside. Which was well furnish with a great big fire place.

The same can be said, about the other cabin which was the idea of a great home. It's been three years since Jason been at this cabin & from his understanding there was no other cabins in the area besides his father's. They would go on to film other things in the area. Like the trail that leds to the lake deep in the woods about a mile from the cabin. That had about eight canoes tie up by the ramp. Which was also new to the area, figuring that it belongs to the owners of the two cabins. Whoever it maybe? It really didn't matter who the canoes belong too? As Jason, Alan & Jerry decided to take it for a spin. They got back to the pier just before night fall when suddenly, they heard strange noises coming from the woods. Just as things couldn't get no stranger on the walk back to the cabin. Jason discovers that the front door of his cabin was open? Considering the fact that he didn't get the chance to unlock it, which was kind of weird in a way. That there were footprints in the dirt leading to the heart of the woods.

Which was also brought to their attention. Which led them to believe that someone else is in the area besides them. Which was kind of creepy in itself as they begin to search the area for answers? Not knowing what's out there waiting on them? They begin to search deep in the woods together. Until that frightful moment when they heard ruckus coming from the bushes that led them to break apart from one another. It was so dark out there that they couldn't see what it was chasing them? Whoever it was? Close in on Jerry's trail very quickly. As he trip & fell over a branch, yelling as if he was be murder to death. That had Jason & Alan thinking the worst at that particular moment. Jason thought that it was the killers coming to even the score with him. That somehow Jasmine & Thomas discover where he was? As it turns out that this wasn't the case at all.

Seemly that Deshawn couldn't help himself. Pulling off a masterpiece with the help of Amanda & Jill who wanted to surprise them. As Jason & his two pals admitted to being scare out of their wits. What a way to get back at her former boyfriend for all the times he scare her in the past.

CHAPTER 6

Camping In The Woods

Jason was relieve once he seen that it was Jill behind the hideous mask. Despite the fact that he had no idea who Deshawn & Amanda was? That threw him off a bit. That had him thinking the worse at that particular moment. Which was all caught on camera by Christian who hid in the woods. Capturing the entire event as one of the best that would go down in history. To finally get one in on Jason as a return favor by using his tricks against him for once. The three of them was stun by the surprise. As Jason & his crew gave them all props for a perfectly good scare. As they all had a great laugh afterwards. It seems as if Jill & Christian arrive around the same time. After Jason & his boys when down to the lake. That led up to this point in time of planning the perfect plot. Thank to his two buddies Jill & Christian. They all then started to exchange hand shakes & hugs by getting to know the new faces in the group. Except for Christian who date hasn't made it yet. The three of them couldn't be more happy to see each other for the first time since that fateful night in October of last year.

They all begin to celebrate by reuniting with one another once again just like the old times. As the three of them begin to chat with each other on how it feels to be together again. As they begin sharing stories about how their lives turn out. Following last year's massacre that took place at Jason's party. Follow by Jason's two camera men who took to the story right from the source itself. As they all gather around the camp fire in order to come up with a solution for the Faces of Death masks. That has impact this entire investigation. Of trying to figure out it's' secrets containing it's involvement in all of this? Which didn't go unattended as Jill & Jason both follow up on the matter & found some interesting things on the internet about the subject. Which was a lot of B.S considering it's true meaning of what it stands for in particular. Containing to a lot of urban legend tales that can be perceive as an indication. As the two of them begin to narrow down the details about certain facts to the stories told?

However, there was one story in particular that caught their attention. The story about how the three masks is use for vengeance that is dish out by someone who is wrong. By using the masks as a warning that whoever receive them is mark for death. Which isn't always the case as each of the three masks represent different quantities in regards of how intense the situation is? That separates the three things that decide's a person's fate. Depending on the mask itself of what's in store for that particular person. Which had everyone on edge about that story as it kind of pertains to them. Not knowing what the cause maybe that had the three of them guessing for answers. Jason on the other hand thought that it was nonsense as he try to change the subject, but the others wouldn't let it go. Being that Jason thought that it was just another stupid urban legend to try & scare them into believing that this is really happening. Thinking that maybe it's something unrelated according to the facts. Of why in the world would Jasmine & Thomas be out killing people for no parent reason.

Which really didn't make no sense do to the fact that Thomas was his best friend & had no reason to do such a thing. Jason believe that there is more to the story than what's been laid on upon them. As he reminded them of the story Eric had told them about how he was set up by the killer. That instantly came across Jill & Christian minds as they also agree with Jason. As for the others who just sat around the camp fire listening in on the conversation. Couldn't believe the story that was being told by the three victims that had them all amaze. Which was all recorded on video by Jason's camera crew. Which was part of the plan to get everyone's insight on what happen. So that they could come up with a solution that would solve this case. They all begin to join in on the conversation to see if they can come up with something. As of how the mind of the killer works. As they took great measures to find the solution the killer is using. By commenting on the urban legends tales in order to obtain certain information about what is going on.

As they begin telling stories about different legendary tales that can be use to benefit the killer. A sudden eerie feeling came over everyone as they discuss the matter. Almost as if they were telling scary stories by the camp fire. Like little troops from a scout club. It seems like the more they when into details about the stories. The more weirder things got as they all started to hear strange sounds coming from the woods. Being out in the opening like that is a sure way of being recognize by all things that lurks within. Including the sounds of footsteps that seems to be creeping around the camp site. It's amazing how the mind can play tricks on a person psyche? When things begin to unravel around them. They all agree to call it a night. Being that it was kind of late. They all rush to the cabin as the wind started to howl? They all was so frighten by the stories being told? That they scare themselves. Being in the woods & all when it's dark out with hardly no light to see what's around them. Made the situation that much unpleasant.

However, it really hit them when they step inside of the dark cabin & turn the lights on. To only come face to face with a girl wearing a hideous clown mask that scare the living hell out of them all. Do to the fact that they wasn't expecting it? Which was sort of a spoiler for them by the party pooper. As it turns out that it was someone arriving early for a party. Instantly, Christian thought that it was Abigail from how attractive she was? Only because he knew that there were no other parties in the area. To their surprise the young lady announce that there is another halloween party. Right next door from them? Which is going to be huge. She then told, "Christian" that he was mistaken, that her name is Lisa? They all were kind of speechless by the breaking news. Considering the fact that they thought they had the area to themselves over the weekend. Which kind of put a dent toward their plans. Knowing that they will now have to share the grounds with foolish teenagers on halloween night.

God knows! what will take place at that party? Which has Jill & the others concern. Which didn't have the same effect on Jason's crew or Amanda & Deshawn who saw the opportunity to attend a real party. It seem as if the three of them didn't want to relive the horror that has haunt them for so long. That the story they told, just might be real. As their friends try to convince them to stay & enjoy themselves for once. That they had nothing to be afraid of? Considering that it was just stories to scare them, just like Jason mention. In which they kind of twisted around, knowing that he was talking about something totally different at the time. As Jason kind of understood where they were coming from. Being that they travel all this way to just end it like that. All because things didn't go the way they planned. So what if there is a party"? Jason had mention to them both. As he explain to them that what's done is done. That there is nothing they can do about it. Except to adapt to the new conditions that has been laid upon them. As Jason quote the phrase that lightning doesn't strike twice in the same place.

Refering to the killers that once had a hold on them, but now it's up to them to let go of the past. That the killers wouldn't dare show up this time around. Considering the fact that the killers had no idea where they are right now. That it would be kind of silly of them to just up & leave like that without the slightest clue of what they think may happened. According to Jason? This was the thing he wanted to avoid. By letting certain things get in the way of their happiness. Through it all, it seem as if the speech work as Jill & Christian sided with Jason. However, it would have seem as if they let Lisa in on their little secret about being the victims in last year's halloween massacre that she pick up on. Lisa couldn't believe that she was standing in the room with the actual victims of last year's on slaughters. Which suddenly made her day, as she had all sorts of questions for them. In which they didn't want to get into at the time. Being that they all just wanted to get a goodnight's rest. Christian, however was in disarray that his date didn't show up yet. So instead, he decided to call her up to see where she is?

Meanwhile, Lisa step out for a moment to get her things out of the car. It seems as if Christian had been stood up by Abigail. Being that her phone went straight to voicemail each time he call. Which kind of broke his heart a little. As Christian had his mindset on meeting the girl of his dreams. Christian then made the suggestion that maybe Lisa could stay with them. Do to the fact that no one is at the other two cabins. Which was all so sudden as Lisa didn't want to oppose herself on them. Being that they didn't know her enough to let her stay. For all they know she could be a psycho killer on the loose. Which was just a thought? As they agree to let her stay the night until her friends show up tomorrow. As the others got ready for bed. Christian decided to stay up with Lisa who was sitting by the fire place. Who could of known that the two of them would hit it off right from the start. The fact that Christian would forget all about Abigail who was now a distance memory. The two of them would go on chatting for hours talking about different things. Then out came the question of the night about the notorious killer who gives a new meaning to the word fear.

Lisa wanted to know how in the world did they survive such a horrible event. Christian try to explain it to her the best way he could, only he didn't have all the answers to the story. Lisa seem very interested in Christian story & promise him that she wouldn't tell a soul. It was around Three'O'Clock when

Christian finally doze off to sleep. While Lisa stood awake to make a phone call. She waited, until everyone was asleep so that she can tell the person on the other end of the call about what is going on. As so she thought that everyone was sleeping as Jason seen her going outside with her cellphone. In which it didn't seem that unusual to him at the time? Thinking that maybe she wanted some privacy. Do to the fact that she didn't want to disturb the others. Jason didn't pay it no mind & went straight to the bathroom. After that, he went back to bed where he stood for the rest of the night.

CHAPTER 7

The Halloween Bash

The next day they all awoke to find that Lisa was missing in action without no explanation on her where'a'bouts. As she was last seen by Jason who saw her going out of the door, early that morning. Thinking nothing of it at the time. Mainly because he was tired & in need of some rest. That all he could think of was the bed. Which seems to be the only thing on his mind at that precise moment in time. Which seems to be very unusual for a person to just walk out like that without telling a soul. The part that really bug them out? Was that it was doing the middle of the night when she departed. That had everyone clueless of what just transpire with a look of uncertainty written on their faces. Trying to figure out just what in the world is going on? That they let someone stay at the cabin who they really didn't know. Which was crazy! they all thought to themselves. Then to top it all off? That made matters worse is the fact that Christian kind of let Lisa in on their little secret. As he reveal everything to her about last year's halloween massacre.

If that wasn't bad enough! Just think how they all felt when they discover that they was being film on Jason's camera. While they all was asleep, thanks! to the note that was left by the computer. Saying that, they all had been expose on camera for what they truly are. As they all seen the video that was left on the computer. Being that they couldn't see who was behind the camera that reveal to them that whoever it was. Wanted them all to know that this person know their secrets that lies within. Claiming that the truth will be recognize within the circle. That each of them is hold accountable for their actions. Which is why this person is doing all of this. In which they didn't take seriously, figuring that it was some kind of joke to humor them. By Lisa who play a prank on them before with the scary clown mask. Which had them thinking de'ja'vu all over again about how their parties use to be. Before all of the nonsense started happening. Things begin to become clear when Lisa enter the cabin with grocery in her hands. Which made all the sense in the world.

By using a little Halloween humor to brighten up the day. All thanks to Lisa who receive a standing ovation from them all. After all, she did reminded them the meaning of halloween. Giving the fact that they had forgotten what it feels like to be in the moment. As they all settle down for a nice big breakfast at the table around back. After breakfast, they decided to get with the program by getting into the halloween spirit. By decorating the cabin with all sorts of creepy things. As they wanted this halloween event to be special. Not long before than the guest started to arrive for the party. Given by the people next door to them. Lisa then introduce the owners of the two cabins to Jason & the others. Being that they are now neighbors. As it turns out that the two cabins belongs to a brother & sister who will be graduating from high school next summer. Who decided to throw this party for their senior class before saying goodbye. Their names were Steven & Kaitlyn.

Which explains why there are two cabins side by side from one another. As one side belongs to the brother, while the other side belong to the sister. Being that they are now neighbors & all. Steven & Kaitlyn both invited Jason & his friends to the party. Jill & Christian decided not to attend being that they already had plans of their own. Even though, they couldn't speak for everyone else. As the others decided that they wanted to be a part of the extravaganza. It seems as if they all couldn't agree on what to do. So Jason told' his two neighbors that the offer is tempting, but they would have to get back with them on the matter. As soon as they could come up with a decision that would benefit them all. With that said'? the argument ensues about the change of plans. As Jason listen to both sides of the argument. In which he kind of understood both cases. On one side Jason could agree with Jill & Christian who didn't want the spot light on them by not drawing attention to themselves. Not telling who is watching them, especially out in the opening like that?

On the other end, Jason could also agree with the others about how one incident shouldn't effect their judgement. Based on how they are behaving? Amanda & Deshawn pleaded with Jill to lighten up a bit & for once have fun. While Lisa try to talk to Christian about joining her at the party. They all just wanted to help the three of them to forget about the past & enjoy life as they should. As hard as it seems for the three of them to let go of what's been done. They all decided to take their friends advice on taking back their lives. As they all raise their glasses to cheer each other on a new beginning. Starting now! At this critical time in their lives, by living it up. As they all laugh in the face of danger. Considering the fact that nothing could go wrong. As they all started to mingle with the folks next door. By getting involve in the activities that was being displayed. Like taking a ride in the canoes or playing games. Which centers around halloween. The fact that everything is going smoothly for now? Without anything bad happening.

Which brings up Jill on the matter who still didn't feel at all safe. Do to the fact that she felt edgy about the whole situation. Feeling as if something wasn't right about how things are going. Almost as if she had a sixth sense about this whole ordeal. Which led her to pay close attention to her surrounding. While Jason & Christian seem as if there is nothing wrong with all of this. As they both was having the time of their lives without a care in the world. With Jason & his crew follow by Christian & Lisa who seems to be connecting on all levels. Regardless of how she feels about certain things. Jill took the initiative to take part in the events with her two friends. Later on that day as time started to past & more people started to arrive at the party. Things started to take a turn for the worse? As Jill receive an unpleasant message on her cellphone from a unfamiliar person. Claiming that things is going to get intense as long as the secret remains hidden within the circle. Which comes with consequences. Which left Jill puzzle about what she just witness & decided to show the message to Jason & Christian. Which was sort of hard to do when you have crowds of people out everywhere's.

As it turns out that it was a false alarm as Jill suddenly remember that it was halloween & that all things applied. Being that tonight, anything go's? As Jill seen all sorts of pranks being play by people. Which is right up Deshawn's alley that was taken in consideration that this is his sort of work. Jill ignore the comments that was made & decided to go with the flow of things. It seems as if Jill wasn't the only one that receive the message. Christian had also gotten the same info as Jill, concerning the same thing. He too brush it off & continue on partying with Lisa. They all was having the time of their lives which was recorded on camera by Jason & his crew. As the three of them was so lucky to capture such a terrific event. The timing of it all was just perfect, as this party hit an all time high. Considering that it is one for the ages. With all of the stuff that is going on. Things that they couldn't imagine in the slights detail. Which is how spectacular this event turn out to be? However, just as things was going smoothly at the party.

In came interrupting was a person claiming that someone has been murder by a psycho killer in a mysterious mask. Instantly, Jason & the others thought of the Faces of Death masks. As they all started to panic, thinking the worse at that particular moment. While everyone else at the party seem worry & concern. As everything around them suddenly stop, as they all witness first hand. The horror of someone staggering from the woods & into the crowd. Where that person would soon collapse to the ground with a knife stuck in his back. The crowd was in total shock from all of the blood that was skidding from his body. That left a eerie feeling in the air that there is a killer in their midst. Just as things was about to get interesting. To the point where everything starts to turn chaotic for everyone. The shock of a life time appear right before their eyes. As the victim risen from the ground & reveal to them all that it was just a prank to get them all work up for nothing.

Which was a cheap thrill to get the adrenaline going as of how they all would react to such a thing. Their reaction resulted to a lot of cheers & applause for a job well done. Which didn't set well with Jill, Jason & Christian who thought the worse at that particular moment. Being that it was kind of childish of them to do. Which wasn't that all funny to the three of them who took it kind of personal. Which was the sort of thing Jill warn them about. On being victimize by their peers of being the target in their little games. Which she try to explain to them. About not being in the spot light. That Christian's little friend Lisa must have told people at the party about their secret. Who is now making a mockery of them by doing this sort of thing. That they had no way of knowing who they were? Until, Lisa came into the picture & reveal who they were. Christian on the other hand disagree with Jill & told her that Lisa wouldn't dare do such a thing. Knowing that she promise him that she wouldn't say a word to anyone about their secret. For all she knows it could of be her two friends Deshawn or Amanda who spill the beans. Knowing that this is how the two of them operate. That they would do anything to get a laugh or two?

CHAPTER 8

Danger Lurks Within

Which cause an arguement between the two of them about who did what? Jason try to play peacemaker by getting in the middle of the conversation to try & see if they could come to a understanding. When suddenly he was thrown in the mix about his two buddies who is filming the whole thing on camera. Who also found it amusing. As they too? Thought that it was great entertainment for the audience. Seeing that there was no point in arguing with each other. The three decided to go their separate ways. Jason & Christian decided to stay at the party while Jill went back to the cabin alone. Just as Jason was headed toward the party to find his two buddies Alan & Jerry. He receive a phone call from a unknown number that supposed to be block. That he wasn't supposed to receive any unknown calls on his phone. Which is kind of weird in a way do to the fact that he was curious to see who it was calling him from a unknown number. Jason found the call to be very unusual when he answer the phone. That someone from the party was trying to manipulate him by pretending to be the killer.

Jason wasn't impress in the least by the threats made by the poser. As he just when along with it, not thinking nothing of it. As he wanted the person to know that he was a good sport. That he can handle a little joke such as this? That he wasn't the type to be scare easily by this sort of thing. Until that is, when the caller got personal on certain details concerning last year's halloween massacre that only the killer knew. That made the situation serious, as all jokes was set a side. As Jason knew that this person means business. From certain stand points by a derange killer who wanted nothing more than to continue what he or she started. Which is to start with the mindgames that seems to get under his skin. As the killer went into details about how he should pay close attention to his surrounding. That he or she could be hiding among the crowd. Just waiting for a chance to strike. That there is all sorts of people wearing costumes. That either of them could be the killers. Not including the pranks that is going on at the party that made things interesting. As Jason seen all sorts of people imitating characters from their favorite scary movie.

Which make things harder to sort out of trying to locate the killer. Which is sort of like finding a needle in a haystack. Jason than became cautious as he try to find Jerry & Alan so that they could help him out on locating the killer. As the killer left him with these famous words before hanging up. Which is just what is his favorite scary movie of all times. That left Jason clueless do to the fact that he had no idea where the killer is? Considering the fact that the killer could be staring right at him for all he knows. That made the situation even harder to bare. Jason suddenly became paranoia as he search for his friends through the harsh crowd. Being that there is all sorts of pranks being play all around him. That had him antsy when someone gets close to him. As he couldn't tell the differents on what is real or not with the stabbing. One thing for sure that made matters worse was that he seen a lot of people on their cellphones making prank calls to others. The idea then pop in his head that maybe he should call Jill on her cellphone so that he can warn her about what is going on.

It seems as if Jason made it some place quiet just before Jill answer her phone. Jill was still kind of upset with the two of them for accusing her two friends of selling out. Based on their background which wasn't right as she explain to Jason over the phone. She then realize that something was wrong based on how Jason is talking. The tone of his voice seem very unlikely? As she ask him," what was wrong & why he seem so upset. "Jason told her, to try & remain calm that he has some very bad news to tell her, but first he ask her. Where is she? Jill told him, that she was in his cabin sitting by the fire place alone. He told her not to move that he will be there in a few. Once he reach Jill at the cabin he told her to brace herself because she is in for a big surprise. That isn't going to be at all pleasant. He told her that the killer is here? Hiding amongst the crowd by blending in as one of the students. Jill was shock by the news as she had a gut feeling that something wasn't right about this party.

Jill explain to Jason that time is at thee essence. That they must warn the others about the danger headed their way before it is to late. Jason suggested that they search the area together as a sure way of not falling victim to the killers plot. Jill & Jason knew that they were taking a great risk by going back into the crowd to search for their friends. Knowing that the killer could be anywhere's. As the killer warn Jason a while ago on the phone that they should be on the look out. Because they are not going to know when or where something would occur. Nor how things is going to turn out. With that said, Jill & Jason found themselves surround by mask killers who purpose was to redefine horror history. In which they witness first hand when someone violently grab Jason from behind & begin stabbing him. The attack was so sudden that Jason didn't know what hit him until it was too late. Jill let out one of the most terrifying screams ever. When she seen Jason go down to the ground in a violently manner. As it turns out that it was just a false alarm. That the person with the knife didn't seem real, as they both let out a sign of relief.

Soon there afterwards! Jill receive a voice message on her phone from the killer. Who can be heard laughing in the background from there little incident that just happen. Who suggested that they be a little more careful from now on. Considering the fact that next time they wouldn't be so lucky. Which only means one thing? Is that the killer has them in site watching them as they take each step. Which places them in a intense situation. However, somewhere's in the middle of the message the killer suggested they play a game call "Dead or Alive? A game that points out the obvious on whether a person lives or not? Which would be entirely up to them on trying to figure out who the killer has in their sites. As the killer went into details about who it is that caught their attention. That soon dawn on them that the killer was talking about Christian who had no idea what is going on. Jill & Jason knew they had to hustle their way to find Christian before the killers get to him first. Somehow, they manage to get separated from one another do to the large crowd.

Jason try desperately to find Jill who he just took his eyes off a second ago. He even try reaching her by phone, but it seems as if all he was getting was a busy signal. So instead he decided to call Christian who life was in danger. It seems as if Jason had a rough time trying to get in touch with him as well. Being that Christian wasn't answering the phone. Which had him worry that something bad must have happened. Thinking that the poor boy didn't stand a chance, which was all Jason could think about. Still in all he didn't give up of trying to find Christian or anyone for that matter. Jason was so focus on finding Christian that he didn't pay attention to anything that is going on around him. Which was a big mistake on his part by not noticing that he was falling right into the killer's plan? By drawing him away from the others so that each of them seem vulnerable to an surprise attack. As the killers had each of them where they wanted them. To seize the opportunity to randomly select a victim. By staying with the game "Dead or Alive" as a way of starting things off.

Jason had a pretty good idea that there was more than one killer in the area, but the problem was he didn't know how many. That whoever it is? Has eyes all over the place, which is troublesome. Knowing that there are eyes following them within the crowds of people attending the party. In which, the killers can blend right in without being discover. Which is the scary part about this whole thing. Having the fear of not knowing what can happened? Which is the thing that will haunt them the most. Meanwhile, Jill seem lost within the crowd of people wearing all sorts of scary masks that seems to have her jumpy each time she turns around. Only to witness the inappropriate behavior of others according to her standards. The poor girl was lost for words as she try to make out who is the perpetrator. Which is mindboggling considering all of the madness that is taking place. Jill seem so out of it, that even the slightest thing such as a grab on the shoulder sets her off. When Deshawn grab her to ask her, where was she hiding out at? Which led to the question of why she is so jumpy? Jill couldn't be more happy to see them. As she starts to explain her situation to them both about why she seem so edgy.

CHAPTER 9

Terror Strikes Again

Jill explain to them that the killers somehow found them & is now on a rampage. Deshawn & Amanda thought that Jill was pulling their chain about how the killer is after her. As they explain to her that it was all in her mind & suggested that she take a look around. Only to show her that she is a victim to someone's joke. Taking in consideration that there is all sorts of pranks being play & that it is halloween. As they told her to get use to it. Jill couldn't stress enough that it wasn't the same as a harmless joke. That she know that it was the real deal only because the killer knew personal things about her that she kept secret. Jill even playback the voice message she receive from the killer. So that they can hear it for themselves. As they still wasn't convince that it was the killer who left her that message. Deshawn couldn't keep a straight face as he bust out laughing. Only because Jill seem so easily convince. Being the prankster that he is? He hip her to the game by explaining the rules to her. That it was them all along with the help of Lisa who pull the same prank on Christian.

They told her that they knew all that stuff about her from Lisa who got the information from Christian the night before. Jill became so furious at them. While at the same time relieve that it was a joke. As Jerry & Alan reveal themselves by emerging from the bushes with the camera's in their hands. Capturing the entire event on video as part of their method to scare them. Jill was still in denial as she told them about the phone call Jason receive. They told her to relax that they pull the same stunt on Jason as well. Then in came Christian with a look of shame on his face. Knowing that he was a victim in their little game. As Jill knew that feeling all so well. Do to the times she been victimize by Deshawn's pranks. As far as Jason goes when they reveal the truth to him. He just totally lost it by wanting to fight as a way to get even. The fact that he didn't find it all that amusing. That it took them all just to get him to calm down a bit. That they didn't mean for it to go this far? Not knowing the seriousness of it. It seems as if though, Jason couldn't stay mad at them for long. Figuring that he would of done the same thing if he was in their shoes.

However, once they got back to the cabin to get a couple of things for the party. They discover that someone spray painted the walls inside of the cabin. In order to relate a message that was written in red that says, "I know your secret"? Instantly, they all turn to their friends thinking that it was one of them that wrote it. As they all seem confuse about who did it? Looking at one another as if they didn't have a thing to do with this. Figuring that maybe it was someone else from the party who did it. However, as they were leaving the cabin. They come to discover the mask of fear hanging on the front door. Which is one of the three masks concerning the faces of death conspiracy? A mask the three knew all so well of what it stands for. Immediately, the three begin to question their friends about the mask & wanted to know who idea was it. To pull this sort of stunt. Which is a slap in the face to the three of them. Do to the fact that it was disrespectful of someone to do this sort of thing. That has them all wondering who would stoop this low just to get their point across. You could almost feel the tension in the room as emotions begin to flare. As the three wanted some answers from their suppose to be friends.

The five of them begin bickering over the matter on who would be stupid enough to do this? Which came down to Deshawn & Lisa who were the prime suspects in this case. Considering there background of not being able to trust either of them. Being that Deshawn blames Lisa do to the fact that it was all her idea in the first place. By leaving him a letter under his pillow the night before on how they should play a prank on the three of them. By describing down every detail on how to manipulate the three of them. By scaring the living hell out of them to let them know the meaning of fear. Which is sort of weird as Lisa denied the allegation on the fact that she wrote a letter saying such a thing. Which led to the camera incident on how she film them all when they were sleeping. In which, she also denied doing. Claiming that she went to the store to to pick up a few items for the party. As they all witness earlier that day. Which seems to stir up constroversy within the group. That led up to the million dollar question which is the arguement. That if it wasn't Lisa who did these things than who was it.

Which had them all wondering about what just transpire, as they try to make sense of it. Which is the part where Jerry & Alan come into the picture. As they try to sort out certain details to the story that would help them understand the situation better. Which led them to believe that someone purposely wrote the letter to Deshawn. Knowing the kind of person he is? By using Lisa signature as a liability to make the letter seem more convincing. Considering that the same person took the camera & film them all. Making it look as if it was Lisa who was behind the camera? Which seems like the only explanation Alan & Jerry could come up with at the time? Which leads them to believe that it's the same person who left this message on the wall. Which led them all to believe that all is not what it seems to be. That there are secrets hidden within the group. That has everyone suspicious of one another. Which seems to be the problem, as this person knew how to manipulate the situation. On how they would react to such a thing. As Jerry & Alan came to the conclusion that this person" Fairly known as the killer. Wanted them to do his or her dirty work. Which is a decoy? So that the killer can unexpectedly arrange a plan to bait them right in.

A plan that causes mayhem & confusion on who is to blame in all of this controversy. Falling right into the killer's plan by making it seem as if there's a traitor amongst them. Which seems to be the case as the message on the wall explains it all? If that wasn't explanatory enough? Then think of how they all must of felt. When they all receive a text message from the killer. Saying that "I Know" refering to the secret that is being held within the group. That had them all convince that someone is withholding information about certain issues. Containing to the killer who knows a secret about one of them. By exposing them all for what they are? That led them to split up in groups to seek out the truth. By going out into the rowdy crowd to search for answers. Which wasn't smart on their part. Knowing that the killer is somewhere's around watching them. The scary thing about this whole situation is that they couldn't make out who was who? With all of the scary costumes that was being worn. That any of them can be the actual killer in disguise. Which makes the search even harder to find the one responsible for all this drama.

The group thing kind of work for a while, as they all begin to lose track of one another. Do to the large crowd of people in attendance at the party. Jill & the others try using their phones to reach each other, but do to the large amount of calls being made in the area. It seem as if all they was getting is a busy signal. As it turns out that it was every man for themselves. Being that each of them must defend for themselves. As Jill would soon get the message as she spotted someone dress like the killer from the movie "Urban Legend". Watching her! As she stare back at the derange psycho killer. Who started to make the first move toward her very quickly. With an ax in the hands of the killer. As Jill didn't waste no time at all by running away. The killer was determine to catch up with her. As the psychopath violently shoved people out of the way to get to her. Jill had no idea where she was running too. As she force her way through the crowd to get as far away from the killer as she possible could. As intensity fill the air each time she look back & seen the killer hot on her trail. By not paying attention to her surrounding Jill had gotten the surprise of a life time.

When she ran into Jerry thinking the worse at that moment. All because she wasn't paying attention to where she was going. Jerry had ask her? What seems to be the problem? Taking that she was in a hurry to get away from him. Jill told him, that the killer is after her. Who is right behind her in a thick over coat. Who seem to drop off the radar when Jerry told her that their is no one there. According to her description. That led Jill to turn around to see that the killer had disappear into the crowd. Which means only one thing is that the killer is buying time to seek out an opportunity to strike when the time is right. As Jill & Jerry didn't feel safe. Knowing that the killer is somewhere's around waiting. So they did what was best? Which is to run to find Jason & Alan who was waiting by the lake. As they made their way through the woods. Jerry & Jill suddenly stop for a brief moment once they spotted the killer searching through the woods for them. As they quickly hid in the bushes before the killer could spot them. It seems as if everything was going to be alright, as the killer had no idea where they were.

Until, Jerry phone started to ring that gave them away, as the killer retreated into the woods. Hoping for a chance to catch them off guard. Jerry desperately try to shut the phone off before the killer could find them. Finally! he got the phone to stop ringing, but the real question was where is the killer. As they begin to look around the trees for anything unusual. Considering the fact that they are all alone in the middle of the woods. Surrounded by trees & thick bushes where the killer could be hiding out at. Leading them to carefully make their way through the woods. Keeping an eye out for any activity. As they move along the bushes. They begin to hear whimpering coming from a certain part in the woods. That suddenly caught their attention as the sound begin to get louder. As they begin to wonder what in the world is making that sound. *They then begin to follow the sound to see what it is? It seems as if the sound was coming from an unknown area. Where there seems to be a lot of trees & bushes. In which they couldn't make out what it was? As they search the area to discover that the sound was coming from a girl who was all curl up in the bushes.*

Who look as if she had been attack by a certain individual who is on the prowl. Jill & Jerry both seem concern that the girl maybe in a state of shock from something horrific. When they try reaching for her, out came rapidly! Through the bushes was the killer wearing something totally different then what they expected. Which was from the movie "I know what you did last summer". A person in a slicker outfit along with a hook that just miss Jerry's face. As the killer went on the offensive by going after Jerry with the hook. It seems as if Jerry was filming the whole thing up until, the sudden attack by the killer. That cause him to drop his camera on the ground. Being that he was under attack. As he was left to face the killer's fury. While, Jill went to check up on the girl who seems to be out of it. When suddenly the girl snap on Jill when she try to help her come too. The girl seem so craze that she pick up a knife to stab Jill. In which she suceed in doing by stabbing Jill multiple of times in the chest. Which turns out to be another practical joke from someone's sadistic personality. That had Jill & Jerry furious of constantly being a pawn in someone's game.

CHAPTER 10

Turmoil

Jill wanted answers of why would they do such a thing. The girl explain to them both that someone suggested that they do this? In order for them to get the message. A message that needed to be deliver to them personally. When suddenly the person in the slicker made it obvious when that certain someone made their presence felt. When it was reveal that the person in the slicker outfit was actually the killer? Who struck down the young lady with the hook. That left her grasping for air moments before taking her final breath. As Jill & Jerry realize that this wasn't a game after all? That they had been fool into believing one thing, when it was something totally different. By the many disguises the killer had recreated throughout the night. That had them guessing beyond reasoning. Not soon afterwards, the killer made the attempt to go after them, as the next target. Jill & Jerry took off like a bat out of hell, leaving behind all of his equipment. The two of them ran wildly through the woods to seek help & notify the others about what is going on. As they both look back & realize that the killer was no where's in site. Taking that this is one of the killer's brilliant concept of the many mindgames being play on them. In which they didn't have no idea what to make of it, as they didn't stick around to find out?

Not soon afterwards, the two manage to catch up with Jason by the lake. Who was standing alone on the pier waiting for Alan to come back. Who went out searching to see if he can find anyone in the group. Which is a huge mistake according to Jill & Jerry who knew better. As they fill Jason in on what the killer is intending to do. That places them all in danger by falling right into the killer's trap. That left Jill & Jason no other alternative, but to search for their friends. Who's lives are in danger? As Jerry stood behind to wait for Alan just in case he makes it back with someone other than himself. Just to be safe? Jill & Jason decided to hold hands, so that they wouldn't get separated again. Meawhile, Christian had no idea that he was being follow by someone with a camera dress in all black like the "Grim Reaper". As he was in search to see if he can find the others. Christian was so focus on the things going on around him, that he didn't notices the killer filming him from a far. The killer follow Christian to the cabin. Where he thought everyone was at? Considering that it is the only place to his knowledge where he would find them.

When Christian reach the front door of Jason's cabin. He notice that someone left him a note that was place on the door. Where he got the message that the killer left for him to read. That said"? What is his favorite scary movie of all time" follow by a camera that was place on him above the door. Which is where the front door would slightly open. Just enough to get his attention that he is being watch. As Christian suddenly got that eerie feeling that instantly came over him. When he slowly open up the door to see who was inside. Christian knew better then to step inside of the cabin. Not knowing what lies waiting on him? As he play it smart by not falling for any of the killer's schemes. Thinking de'ja'vu all over again from the night in the Galleria hall where he was deceive by a lie. Just as Christian lean in the doorway to take a peek inside. He seen a shadow figure move behind the door. As if someone was waiting patiently for him to step inside. Which led him to back away slowly, in order to not tip the killer off that he is aware about what's happening? Just as Christian turn around to run away. He suddenly came face to face with the killer who was standing behind him. That literally scary him half to death? Which was a spur of the moment kind of thing. Which is something he wasn't expecting to happened?

As the killer didn't waste any time at all with the assault on Christain, as he try to defend himself. That instantly became an all out brawl. As Christian was in the fight of his life. Against an aggressive killer who wouldn't stop at nothing to claim another life. Somehow, Christian manage to slip away from the killer's grasp, but not without a few wounds to show for. Yet he still wasn't free from the horror as another killer appear from behind the door. Dress in one of the faces of death outfit that led to the chase. As Christian did everything in his power to avoid the machete the killer had as a weapon. That landed him on the roof of Jason's cabin. Where the killer would disappear from site. Once they heard Jason & Jill's voice in the distance. Christian was relieve to hear the sound of their voice. As he climb down from the roof to meet them. They all met in front of the cabin where they spotted the two costumes that the killers had on. Which was place inside of the trash can. Where they discover one of the faces of death masks. Which states the message that the stage has been set for their demise. A message that they knew all so well of how it effects the outcome according to the the mask description.

That had the three of them wondering what the killers have in store for them now. Considering the fact that the killer is full of surprises. Now that he or she has thee upper hand on things. As they had a hard time trying to figure out who is the killer with the many faces that is being using to confuse them. Not to mention having other people do their dirty deeds for them in order to create turmoil on who they believe is the killer. With all of the pranks that is being play didn't make things any easier to sort out. As they all took it in consideration that the one's that is pranking them could indeed be the killers for sure. As they begin to question each other on how well they know their friends. That the killer is blackmailing someone from the group. By having them do things in order to keep that person's secret from being reveal? Which sort of make sense of why the killer would write such a thing knowing the consequences that may follow one's actions. By taking orders from the killer to do whatever needs to be done. In order to fulfill his or her quota as a statement to the three of them. Which led them to believe that one of their companions is hiding a dark secret that needs to be expose.

Their focus now is to get to the bottom of this conspiracy. In order to seek out the truth. So they can have a better understanding about what is going on? By getting someone from the group to admit the truth. As they were getting ready to leave to find their friends. The three of them manage to run into Kaitlyn who was just the person they needed to talk too. About the current situation that needs to be address. By revealing the truth to her about who they really are & that she needs to shut down the party right away. To avoid any further killing in tonight's event since she was half responsible for everyone's well being. Jason suggested that she wait for them in his cabin. Only because they didn't have the time to explain it to her at the moment. Kaitlyn agree to the terms do to the fact that she was fascinated by their story. The three of them continue on to see if Alan had return to the lake. Somewhere's between the lake & the cabin. Christian suddenly got distracted by a phone call from the killer. Who let him in? On a little secret about who is the next target. By describing certain details on who it is? That led Christian to believe that the killer was talking about Kaitlyn who was all alone in the cabin.

Which didn't make no sense as of how the killer would slip right by them without being notices. Being that they just left the cabin a second ago. That he was positive that no one enter the cabin behind Kaitlyn. In which he was mistaken? As the killer reveal to him that they didn't have to sneak into the cabin. When in fact, they never left the cabin to begin with. As the killers had Christian fool by having him believe that they had left the cabin? That by placing the two costumes in the trash can. Would have them thinking that the two killers had fled the scene. Once they heard Jill & Jason voice. When actually the two never left & that the costumes was just a diversion. To throw them off? By pulling the oldest trick in the book. At that point? Christian rush to Kaitlyn's aid. Hoping to reach her in time before the killer does? When Christian reach the cabin he found that the door was lock from the inside & that there was no other way to get in. Instead he decided to yell out Kaitlyn's name. Who has no idea what was going on? However, when she open up the window. That was located upstairs inside of the cabin. Christian did everything he could to warn her about the danger headed her way, but it was a little too late.

As the killer snuck up behind her with a razor sharp knife & violently went to stabbing her. If that wasn't bad enough! The killer would go on to throw her out the window. With a rope tie around her neck that instantly snap from the force in which she was thrown. The killer then try to imtimidate Christian by sliding the knife across his or her neck. Christian immediately went to seek help from anyone who was available. To show them the horror that has ascended upon them. His main focus was to find Kaitlyn's brother, "Steven" to give him the heads up about his sister's death. Instead, he found two police officers who was patrolling the area at the time. Christian couldn't be more happy to see them. As he broke down every detail about what's been going on. That they should be on the look out for a psycho killer who is on the loose. Who is wearing the costume from the movie "Urban Legends" who is set out to kill. By displaying different characters from the horror movies in order to create chaos. By using the crowd as a certify way to blend in with all of the scary stuff that is going on. As he advise them to not take any of this lightly?

The police took down his information about the description of the killers costume. Strangely enough, he didn't have a face to go along with the description *of the person behind it all. Which seems to be a problem for Christian who had no idea who it is behind the mask. Which isn't much of a case when there's no description of the killer. The police ask? "Christian" was there any more evidences he would like to share with them? Which brought Christian's attention to Kaitlyn's lifeless body that was thrown from the window. Thinking to himself that if this doesn't convince the police to shut down the party, then nothing will. What a turn of events as the situation became unbearable to withstand. That made Christian out to be a liar? As there was no sign of Kaitlyn's body anywhere's to be found. That instantly had the police talking about how Christian misled them. Which is a huge mistake for Christian. As the police place him under arrest for making a false claim. Just as the police was getting ready to take him away. In came poping up was Jason & Jill along with his crew & Lisa. As they wanted to know why was Christian in handcuffs. As Jill explain to the police that they are arresting the wrong person. That the killers is still out there watching them from a distance. All of the commotion that was going on between them. Brought a bit of a surprise when Amanda & Deshawn step out of the cabin?*

CHAPTER 11

The Danger Zone

With a note they receive from someone at the party explaining how they are blinded from the truth. That the answers they seek lies within? Which may not be the answer they are searching for. By unmasking the truth behind the mystery that follows. According to how they are perceive that makes things interesting. On how well they know one another that really going to capture their attention. By the sudden responds given by them all. As a sure way of showing someone's true colors. When the pressure is on? That had everyone under suspicion. That led the police to intervene in the discussion. As they decided to look into the case by calling for backup. The two policemen suggested that they all stay together in order to avoid anymore controversy. As they follow the police orders to stay in doors, until they get some sort of idea of what is going on? Once in the cabin they all begin to bicker over the matter. As Jason became highly upset that either of them wouldn't come clean. That led each of them to go their separate ways. As Jill & Jason realize the sudden mood change of Lisa? Who attitude seem to change when the subject came up about a secret. Christian didn't see it that way, as he explain to them both that the poor girl is terrify.

Do to the situation she is in, which is kind of understandable considering the circumstances. However, it would have seem as if Jason started to consider everyone as a suspect. Not including Jill & Christian as a liable source. As he put two & two together by narrowing down the details about each of them. Like for instant, how Amanda is so quiet that it state's the obvious on where she stands. Not knowing what's going on in that mind of hers. Which goes to show someone that you can't trust a person like that? No telling what is on her agenda, as of how a person can appear to be? Considering her innocent's that creates a disturbance. On the other hand there's a trickster who loves to play games with people. In order to seek out the worse in a person. By all means to satisfy his desires of making a statement when it comes down to scaring someone. That easily places Deshawn as a target do to how he is perceive as a prankster. Which so happens to be what the killer is doing to confuse them. Into believing one thing, when it is something totally opposite then what they expected.

That ties Deshawn as a possibility according to his behavior that seems a bit odd. Considering his love of scaring people in which he does best. That had Jason concern on the matter, which left him with a huge decision to make. On whether Amanda & Deshawn are the suspects in the killers plot. Considering their bond of how unique they can feed off one another's ambition. Considering their aggression toward others that makes them dangerous to be around. Which is the type of thing Jason notices about the two of them. That there is more to the story that meets thee eye with the two of them. Last, but not least, the moral of the story that creates so much controversy within the group. Has to deal with Lisa who just appear out of nowhere's as a spectator. Who stumble upon their little secret by accident, "thanks" to Christian who reveal a little more than he should of have. Taken into consideration that they didn't have any information on who she is? Nor where she came from? That begs the question? On who is this Lisa girl? That has befriended them. As Jason had to answer the million dollar question about Lisa's motive.

That had him worry that Lisa is withholding information from them all. Which can be fatal considering what the secret is? That only the killer knows of? Which is bad news for them all. Thinking to himself that nothing good can come from this? As he suddenly realize that everyone has some sort of dark secret they are hiding. Which makes the situation even harder to bare with? Taken that no one wants to bring up their dark past. Which is the kind of thing the killer feeds off. By exploiting one's hidden secret & use that as advantage over a person. Who is weak minded to such a thing. Taking that the person is willing to do anything to remain undetected. Which goes for everyone, including Jason? Who started to question himself on things he may have done in the past. As Jason, himself was in denial about certain issues that was brought to his attention. As the tension in the room was so thick that you can almost feel the hostility. As if they all was thinking the same thing about one another. Which brings up a good point considering how they are perceive that makes them all look guilty. According to Jason who is showing a bit of concern. About who can he trust at this point not knowing what's at stake.

At that point Christian & Jill could see the fear in Jason's eyes, that something wasn't right. A look of uncertainty that says it all went paranoia takes affect. Still in all? He remain calm in light of the situation. Christian on the other hand did some thinking on his own. About how Deshawn & Amanda emerge from the cabin without running into the killer who was inside. Who supposedly receive a note from someone at the party. Which is sort of complicated when things don't add up. As of how someone would randomly hand them a note explaining the situation. When the two of them appear in the cabin where the killer had been all along. Which instantly reminded him that he had forgotten all about Kaitlyn's body. That could be hidden inside the cabin. Thinking that the killer didn't have time to dispose the body right then. Which was a stupid thing to not mention when the two policemen ask him? Was there any evidence he would like to show them. A mistake he will soon regret for not noticing at the time. Figuring that the answer to all their problems was sitting right under their noses the whole time. Just then, at that precise moment, the cabin went completely dark. As the lights in the cabin shut off.

Chaos was beginning to spread throughout the cabin, as they search for a way out. There were all sort of stuff being knock over that had them all jumpy. Not knowing who will they encounter along the way of finding a opening. Then all of a sudden! They heard a scream that came from by the stairs? That led to a lot of noise of things being knock around. Which sounded like a scuffle? They couldn't tell who it was being attack do to the darkness. As they scramble their way through the darkness to search for the place where the noise was coming from? Which is sort of hard to do when there are screams all around them of mistaken identity. By them running into things thinking that it's the killer? Just think? Of all the stuff they encounter trying to feel their way through the dark cabin. Which is a sure way of falling victim to the mind games being play by the killer. About a secret one of them is carrying. Which only make matters worse do to their current situation. Then finally, the lights cut back on? As everything became silent, as if nothing had happen. They seem amaze of how far apart they were from one another. As they soon discover where the noise was coming from? Which was just a reaction from them running into stuff. Mistaking it as the killer? Not long before than Alan came stumbling down the stairs. With blood on his shirt & pants from being stab multiple times.

They all rush to his aid to see how bad off he was & to see if they could assist him in any way. His injuries, however was not life threating, although he suffer some inflicting cuts to the body. Alan seem out of it, as if he no longer felt safe around them. Claiming that it was one of them who attack him when the lights shut off. Pointing to the area where he seen the coat hanging up on the rack. That the killer had on when he was attack, which was from the movie "Urban Legends". Christian thought that it was preposterous, as he explain that there was no way the killer could of just slip on the coat without being notices. Which didn't make no sense what so ever of how the killer would randomly select him. When the killer had multiple choices to choose from. Adding to the fact that it was too dark to sort out anything. Even for the killer who just crept by everyone in order to get to him, which was a joke in itself. As a argument ensued between Christian & Alan on the matter. Which is getting in the way of the real subject on who it was that attack him in the first place? That needs to be address immediately before discussing any other issues.

CHAPTER 12

Playing The Victim

Everyone became suspicious of one another as they all started to point fingers. On who they think is responsible for the attack on Alan. That the secret just might be hidden within the group. Only to discover that the killer might be hiding amongst them who knows the secret that lies within one of them. Which sort of make things interesting as certain issues play itself out. That cause them all to misbehave irrationally over something that is totally beyond their understanding. Which makes things complicated to sort out, as the plot thicken's. As they all made strong points about one another that made the situation more intense. As they narrow down the facts of certain clarification. That led them all to believe that the two suspects is no one other than Deshawn & Amanda? Based on their perception of how everything seems to connect to them. As their reputation ensues them of being pranksters. Even though, Amanda acts as if she wasn't part of the scam that is being played on them. As Deshawn once again defended Amanda, as he always do? According to Jill who suspected nothing less. Of why Amanda won't fend for herself? That she always have Deshawn come to her rescue, which seems a bit odd.

Things seem to get worse for the two of them as Christian & the others started to pull up more dirt on them. That had Jill wondering about the two of them. As Christian explain to them that Amanda & Deshawn was in the cabin the whole time since he arrive on the scene. Who by the way roughen him up a bit. When he encounter them earlier in that very same spot. Who also kill Kaitlyn right before his eyes. As the two of them try to convince them all that the killer is setting them up to take the fall. By using them as bait, do to the fact that they was caught leaving the crime scene. While the police was present.

Deshawn try to be as straight as he possibly could? When he explain that the killer is trying to frame the two of them. With the note explaining that their assistance is needed immediately at the cabin. However, when they arrive at the cabin. They rush inside to see what is going on? Only to discover that no one was inside of the cabin at the time. That led the two of them back on the porch where they spotted them all with the police. Which still didn't add up according to them. Do to the fact that the killer is among them. Pretending to be friendly. Which create's so much controversy between them.

For all they know Amanda & Deshawn could of written the note themselves in order to cover their tracks. Just as they did before when Deshawn try to blame Lisa for the note he receive early on. Explaining how they should come up with a plan to scare Jill, Christian & Jason by playing a joke on the three of them. Which seem meaningless at the time only to uncover the truth on what their true intention are? Deshawn stuck with his story no matter who believe them. That had the two of them despising Jill for not supporting them. Just as things begin to unravel. In comes another surprise that made the situation even worse to analyzes. When they all receive a picture mail on their cellphones. Showing a picture of Amanda & Deshawn with Jasmine & Thomas? If that wasn't bad enough? Then just think of how the three of them must of felt when the message stated that the four of them were friends. That created a whole new outlook on things. Of how intense the situation became when the truth was finally reveal. Which left the three of them stun by the sudden turn of events. That landed Amanda & Deshawn in the hot seat for some explaining.

As Jason & Christian demanded answers from the two of them about the picture. Concerning the four of them being friends, which needs to be address right a way? Jill on the other hand felt as if she was deceive by the two of them. As her suspicion of them, finally adds up. Do to certain details that come to mind, like how they set this whole thing up. Being that Jasmine & Thomas must have encourage the two of them to step in on their behalf. By doing whatever it takes to get the three of them together again. So that they could finish what they started one year ago. Which explains the secret behind Deshawn & Amanda's actions. Of how they down play this whole thing. In order to carry out Thomas & Jasmine plans of wait until the opportune time to strike again. Which explains the sudden change of costumes that is being display. By the four of them who is taking turns killing people. In order to confuse them by thinking one thing, when it is something totally different.

Deshawn became furious when he seen everyone accusing them of a crime. He & Amanda didn't commit. As they try to paint a picture of them that is misleading on all angles.

The two of them became so outrage that they didn't feel the need to explain anything to them. As they both storm out of the cabin with a chip on their shoulders. Jill try taking off behind them, but she was stop dead in her tracks by Jason. Who suggested that this is what they want her to do? That she know first hand what they are capable of? Jason is willing to bet his top dollar that the two of them are in on the scheme the killer has set. Only because he can see right through them, as suppose to their reaction. When face with reality that results to them leaving. Jill try to point out the obvious that there is a possibility Amanda & Deshawn might be telling the truth. According to Eric's story about him being set up by the killers whoever it maybe. That this just might be another of the killers plans to throw them off? As she reminded Jason about his situation last year on how he must of felt when the killers try to frame him. Christian however, disagree with her on the subject. As he swore that it was the two of them who attack him eariler & murder Kaitlyn in the process?

This he can vouch for? Knowing that their was no one who could of slip in or out of the cabin. Within the few seconds he went to seek help for Kaitlyn. Which was just a couple of seconds before he ran into the two policemen. In which he return with the two officers back to the cabin. It would seem as if the killers wanted the police to think that Christian was trying to pull one over on them? By getting them to believe that there's an actual killer in the area. Considering all of the pranking that is going on. Which led the police to believe that it is all part of the halloween tradition. Which was a sure way for Deshawn & Amanda to downplay the whole thing. By making it relevant the moment they step foot outside the cabin? Only to play with each one their intelligence by coming up with some lame excuse. To cover their tracks? Which is why they came forward knowing that they were about to be exposed? Knowing that if they play dumb to the fact that they showed up at the cabin. At the wrong place, at the wrong time. Then it would look sort of like a misunderstanding? Which is why the two of them killed Kaitlyn because she probably got a good look at their faces. Which left them no other choice, but to kill her. In doing so, the killers decided to make note of it, by calling him. It would seem as if Christian has a good instinctive about Amanda & Deshawn. According to Alan? Who believe's it was one of them who attack him. Jill could also argue the fact that Amanda & Deshawn could of arrive at the scene moments after he left to find help. That eventually led him to the police. In that case? Christian answer Jill's question with a question of how the two of them didn't run into the killers at that point.

Which seems kind of odd considering that they didn't encounter anyone in the short time he was gone. Which would answer the million dollar question about Amanda & Deshawn on whether they encounter someone & if they did what was the circumstance. As they debated on whether Jasmine & Thomas is the master mind behind the killing. Which seems kind of ridiculous considering that they all was once friends. Which makes the situation hard to believe. Then again, it could be a possibility? Considering how things went down at the Hall that night. Which stir up a lot of confusion on the matter about their sudden disappearance. That left a big question mark for them to consider. As the games played by the killer continues to haunt them. As they couldn't make heads or tails on what the picture means in regards to how it is portray. Christian remain cautious by not falling for another one of the killers scams. As he knew first hand what the picture means? That there was no getting around the fact that the four of them are full of deception. By misleading them from seeing the truth?

Which is the question that is troublesome to this whole ordeal that maybe the people they consider friends. Is not at all what they seem to be? That the picture tells it all? By searching for an answer that would solve this conspiracy? When the answer they were looking for? is right under their noses. According to Christian? Who took the time to think this thing over. Jill still wasn't convince by Christian's theory. According to how he presented his case. Jason seem confuse by the entitle situation as he couldn't make up his mind on who to believe. While his two buddies along with Lisa wanted nothing more than to get to the bottom of it. Figuring that it would make a great story for the public? Just as things couldn't get no weirder. Jill receive a video on her phone that was sent to her by a certain individual. Who wanted nothing more than to get her attention by showing a video of her two friends. Amanda & Deshawn who seem as if they are being follow by someone. Which make things interesting only because the two of them had no idea that they are being follow. Things instantly got intense for Jill as she show the video to the others.

CHAPTER 13

Taking Precaution

Who found the video to be very disturbing as of how critical the situation became. As they all witness first hand the horror that follows Amanda & Deshawn every move. Things had became intense at that very moment. Knowing that they would have to do something. In order to save the two of them from being the killers next target. Just as Jill was getting ready to leave? Christian had pointed out the concept. That something seem fishy about this whole setup containing to the video. Stating that it is all a front to lure them out into the opening. Where they would be vulnerable within the crowds of people. Not knowing what to expect to happen? When there is obviously something wrong with this picture. He simply reminded them of the picture that was taken of the four of them together. As Christian came up with the conclusion that this is all part of their plan. By thinking that the two of them are in serious danger. Only to lure them out amongst the crowd so that Jasmine & Thomas could knock them off one by one. Which created a problem amongst them even though Christian made some good points. Which is just the thing that concerns them that puts them in a bit of a bind. Only because they didn't have a clue on whether Amanda & Deshawn was in danger or not that puts a spin on things.

Which takes them back to that night in the Galleria hall where they had to make decisions based on the truth or dare games. Where a decision had to be made? Which is the thing that now has to be consider if they want to know the truth about the two of them. Which is a bit of a gamble by risking their lives to seek out the truth. Which is kind of intriguing according to Lisa who is amaze by all this chaos. As the adrenaline suddenly became a factor do to the thrill of the hunt. Which is sort of fascinating to their three friends who saw the opportunity to end this madness once & for all. That now is the time for Alan & Jerry to put their skills to the test by seeking out the killers. Which gave them an idea that if they are going to search for Amanda & Deshawn? They will have to be smart about it, by splitting up into groups of three's. That way they would stand a better chance of not falling victim to the killers gameplan. Lisa had suggested that maybe Jill, Jason & Christian could search together as a group. While she tag along with Alan & Jerry on the hunt for Amanda & Deshawn. Christian, however didn't want to be included in the group & decided to stay at the cabin. Only as a precaution do to the circumstance.

Instead Jill & Jason went together to see if they could find Amanda & Deshawn in the large crowd of people in attendances. The hunt was now on? It was just the question if they could reach them in time before the killer does? As they both got the feeling that something doesn't feel right. Five minutes into the search. That sudden eerie feeling came over them. Thinking that they too are being watch from a distance by the killers. Who is probably stalking them as well, following their every move. It didn't matter how hard they try to maintain their composer. They still couldn't shake the feeling of being watch under close supervision. At that particular moment? Jill & Jason both receive a phone call from the killer who put them on a three way call. So that he or she can stir up more controversy by doubling the fun. At that moment? Jill & Jason realize that they had made a huge mistake. By falling right into the killer's trap just as Christian predicted. Instead of crying over spill milk the two decided to make good of the situation by not letting the killer get to them. Which is exactly what the killer is trying to do by getting inside of their heads with the mindgames.

It didn't matter how hard they try to ignore the comments made by the killer. The fact of the matter was that the mindgames is now starting to take it's affect upon them. As the killer got down & dirty with the two of them by doing whatever it takes to get their attention. Which seems to be working as the killer struck a nerve by constantly pushing their buttons. Knowing that they are being watch by the killer? Jill & Jason both begin to search through the crowd to see if they could find the person on the other end of the call. Which seems impossible? According to the many prank calls that are being made by the people surrounding them. That landed them in a situation that is impossible to get out of? As the killer had them in place to begin the torment. The danger rate begin to rise as they started to be a part of everyone's joke. Do to the fact that they were amongst the rowdy crowd. Who would randomly select someone in the crowd to prey upon. Which gave the killer the upper hand on things. As Jill & Jason had no idea what direction the killer was coming from? Nor when the attack would take place.

That left the two of them questionable about their surrounding based on who amongst the crowd is the actual killer. The two of them was constantly being victimize by other people's pranks. That had the two of them jumpy each time it happens. As the killer didn't make things any easier by baiting the situation. Causing them to believe the hype that something can instantly transpire within the crowd of people. Something simply as a little prank could end up bad for them. Do to the fact that they are not going to know when it's coming. That they are not going to suspect a thing until it happens. The mindgames was in full effect as the killer instructed them on whether they are getting hot or cold. Based on how close they are to Amanda & Deshawn? The deal with this sort of thing is that they would have to go by what the killer says. Which could end up one or two ways? The pressure was now on? As of how this thing would play out. Perhaps it could be that the killer is leading them right into a trap or toward something far much worse. Taking into consideration that they would have to be extremely careful not to be pawn in the killer's game.

These are the sort of things that could drive a person mad by all of the little mischievous mischief that they have to put up with. That creates stress on the brain according to how to deal with the pressure the two of them are under. Having to deal with all of the confusion that the killer is putting on them. The goal was to distract the two of them from the main objective. Which is to draw the attention away from the source itself? Which was staying alert of the killer who is roaming through the crowd. To focusing all their attention on finding Amanda & Deshawn who holds the key to the solution. What a huge mistake that was? As the killer place them in the thick of things where the plot would surfaces. When they spotted someone in a scary goblin costume who seems suspicious. That had the two of them wondering just what is this person's true intention. Which led them to believe that it is probably the killer by the way this person is acting. Strangely & yet odd, is the only way to describe how ironic it all seems. As they try to figure out what this person deal is? On why this particular person is behaving out of the ordinary.

Which had their full attention based on this person's actions that had them curious. Not realizing the danger that is lurking within the shadows. Who is silently creeping up behind them. As their focus was all on the goblin. Which seems to be a diversion to take their focus elsewhere's. Distracting them so that the killer could make his or her move. Just as the killer was about to make a move. Jill spotted the person from the corner of her eye. Within that split second? Jill took off running with the killer in pursuit. Jason had no idea what just transpire as he seen Jill take off running through the crowd. Just as he was about to go after her? The person in the goblin costume grab a hold of Jason & yank him back. Almost as if the killer was pulling him away from going after Jill. Who had other plans in store for him. Which almost seems like a well thoughtout plan to separate the two. In order for their trap to work. Somehow, Jason manage to escape from the killer's grasp. By putting up a fight against the aggressive killer. Who would stop at nothing to claim his life as well. Once free from the killer's grip. Jason didn't waste anytime going after Jill to assist her. Jill on the other hand is face with a serious problem as the killer was hot on her trail.

By not paying attention to her surrounding. Jill manage to bump into Deshawn as the two collided with one another. Jill didn't realize that it was Deshawn she had bump into? Do to the fact that her main focus was on the killer. Who seem persistent on getting to her. All she could do is scream as loud as she possibly could hoping to get someone's attention. Do to the circumstances that things didn't turn out the way she expected. As it turns out? That the person in the hideous costume wasn't after her. The killer just made it look that way by playing games with her over the phone. That the person chasing her was after someone else at the party. The fact of the matter was that she was caught in the middle of a crosshair. As the killer couldn't resist the temptation of spicing things up a bit. By displaying the true meaning of fear? Of not knowing what to expect when the pressure is on. Jill's tolerance begin to wear thin? As she could hear the killer on the phone laughing hysterically? Jill then became furious over the matter & ended the call. Within seconds, Jason arrive on the scene where an argument ensued between him & Deshawn. Things had gotten so intense between the two of them that they lost sight of what's important.

CHAPTER 14

Surviving The Game

Just within the matter of minutes disaster strikes when the killer targeted Jason. Who is unwear of the killer's presence at the time. As the killer took aim at Jason with an ax while wearing the costume from the movie Urban Legends. The killer would miss him by inches do to a little interference. From Amanda who shove him out of the way in time to avoid the swinging ax? Even though, the same couldn't be said about her. As Amanda put her life on the line to save him. Which goes to show them that they are not the one's responsible for what has been taking place as of late. With regards to them being the killers. It all happen so fast that the three of them didn't see it coming. Do to all of the commotion that is going on between Jason, Deshawn & Jill. Who try to stop them from fighting. It was a last minute decision on Amanda's part by stepping in when she notice that something was wrong. Amanda then fell into Deshawn's arms, as they both fell to the ground. She die almost instantly from her wounds. While the killer escapes yet again within the crowds of people. They try to get some help from the people around them, but they all was to drunk or loaded to realize anything. As they all took it to be some sort of joke as a way to psych them out.

Jill, Jason & Deshawn realize that now they are on their own from here on out. As they try to make it back to the cabin where it is safe. While holding on to Amanda's lifeless body to give her a proper burial. Even though, they still would have to be on the look out for the killers who is lurking within the crowd. Which makes things even harder to focus on? Knowing that something can instantly happen within the matter of seconds. The mindgames started to take affect on the three of them. As the thought kept running through their minds about the sudden fear of having watchful eyes all around them. Of not knowing what will they encounter when face with absolute chaos. Knowing that they are in unfamiliar territory by being in the center of the mayhem. Which makes them a target in the heat of things. That creates a opening for the killers who is carefully planning their next move. That eventually led to the message the killer left for them to read. Which was posted on Jason's cellphone. As a warning, that they need to pay close attention to their surrounding. Considering that the killers are in hot pursuit of following in their footsteps. As the killer ask them? Could they feel heat that is bearing down on them. Closing in, on their position, as they speech? Almost instantly, they became alert to their surrounding.

Reacting with such urgency to the cause that had the three of them concern about the people in general. Making things all so complicated to resolve. Which is sort of hard for them to do when carrying around a dead body. To make the situation less complicated they lay down Amanda's body on the ground & form a circle around her. As they try to make out who amongst the crowd is the killer. As they all knew that they couldn't rely on instinct alone. Follow by the current costume the killer had worn. Despite the fact that the killer may have change into another costume. Which makes the situation even more difficult to analyze. By putting them in a awkward position. Of staying alert to every little detail that is perform around them. As the killers wanted to make a statement that would leave the three of them stun on what is about to take place. When someone from the crowd announce to everyone who was listening. That there has been a murder. Fearing the worse at that particular moment they all gasp silently. Expecting something real horrible from the crime scene that would shed some light on what has been taking place. All the while they were partying? That led Jill & Jason to intervene in the conversation to give some insight on the recent murders.

As the crowd was in absolute disbelief of the story that has been laid upon them. About a craze killer on the loose that is set out to kill. Who by the way, is fascinated with famous slashers from the horror movies. Which involves around three mysterious masks that connect together as the source behind the constant change of costumes being display by the killers. With that out of the way? The party goers could finally understand where Jill & Jason was coming from? As they all wanted to know more about the legendary Faces of Death masks. Which brought their attention to the dead body found by a certain individual attending the party. As it turns out that this hold ordeal was nothing more than a hoax to terrorize the people who brought into the story. A story that backfire in Jill & Jason faces by the crowd of people who applaud the two of them for getting everyone else all work up. By a tremendous performance from the two of them. That their expression says it all? That the two of them seem so convincing that it almost seems real in the eyes of the audience. Jill & Jason couldn't believe the responds they had gotten from the crowd. As the killer made the two of them look like total fools in front of everyone. When they try to convince the crowd that their friend had been murder. By showing them Amanda's body that suddenly turn up missing.

As it turns out that this hold senseless act was nothing more than a distraction. To keep things in perspective so that the killers can remain conceal within the crowd & to also get rid of the evidence by disposing Amanda's body. The three of them seem clueless about what just happen. As they try to make sense of it all. Of how the killers manage to give them the slip once again. In doing so, they manage to take away Amanda's body in the process. Taking away their one true indication that proves there's a killer among them. All seem lost? Until, Deshawn spotted one of the killers in the Urban Legends gear. Draging something that seem like a body wrap in a brown sack. The three of them seem curious & wanted to know who or what is inside of the sack. As they begin to follow the mysterious character in the trench coat at a safe distances to see where he or she is headed. They follow this person deep in the woods where the noise from the crowd seem very distance. To the point where everything seem unfamiliar to them. Unaware of Jill, Jason & Deshawn's presence. The killer continue on doing what he or she does best. Which Jill suddenly pick up on, as the thought enter her mind that this person is fully aware of their presence.

Who is successfully drag them into another one of their many schemes to lure the three of them in unexpectedly. As so they thought? Taking that they couldn't make heads or tails on whether this is part of the plan or not. Deshawn didn't care whether this was a trap or not. All he wanted was payback for Amanda who took the fall for them. Without thinking twice about it? Deshawn in a heated rage went after the killer to end this thing once & for all. Jill & Jason would soon follow to catch the killer in the act. They would soon find out that it was a false alarm. When they found out that it was just a manikin stuff with candy that was place inside of the sack. Sort of like a *pinata? As it turns out that this was all a mistake, as the killer led them on, under false pretense. Which led them to the hidden camera's up in the trees. Which explains everything from here on out. Which led them to believe that whoever is behind the camera is responsible for everything that has happen so far? Which is the reason why the killers seem to know all about what is going on. Whether it's spying on them or knowing their exact location at the party. For once, things begin to unravel as the three of them finally caught on to what the killer is doing.*

That led them on a hitting spree by smashing all of the cameras with a bat. That suppose to be use for the human like pinata, which seems to be the only thing they can find to get rid of the cameras. Except for the fact that there will be no candy falling from this gadget. They then headed back to the cabin to regroup, as they also got rid of the camera that was hung in front of Jason's cabin as well. Once inside of the cabin they begin to search the place for anything unusual & discover that Christian is missing. Which led them to believe one or two things in result to this misdemeanor. In which they can look at it, one or two ways. One being that the police had return with backup & needed Christian's assistance to bring forward the killers. The other being that Christian had gotten a unexpected visted from someone in particular who saw the chance to take him out. Which turn out bad either way you look at it. Do to the fact that the killers have eyes all around the camp site. Who is aware of everything that has gone down. As they couldn't help but to feel out of sync. Do to the fact that the killers are always two steps ahead of them each time. Considering that they couldn't make out the situation involving Christian's disappearance.

As they struggle to figure out just what is going on with all of the confusion that is taking place. Then at that precise moment! Jill receive a text message from Christian who wanted to know their location. Explaining that he got her stress call that they needed his assistance Asap? Jill seem confuse by the message & text him back that she did no such thing. In regards, to her senting him anything of that nature. She then realize that this was no coincidence? That this has the killers name all over it. Which led to the real question of how the killer manipulate Christian. By having him to believe that Jill & Jason got a hold to the police. Not knowing that it was the killer who is behind this whole ordeal. As Jill quickly sent him a text explaining his situation. The only problem was that she didn't know if he got her message. Do to the fact that her phone die. Just as the message was being sent to him. Time was at the essence as the three of them scramble their way through the crowd in search for him. The question was? If they can reach him in time before the killer does?

CHAPTER 15

Crossroads

They seem to have a big problem on their hands, while in search for Christian. Being that they didn't have a clue on Christian's where'a'bouts. Which is the question that bothers them the most on whether this is a setup to lure them out into the opening. Where the killers has the advantage by using the crowd as a liability to blend in. With the many different scary costumes that is being displayed. While on a killing spree? Which is unnoticeable to the crowd. Considering that everyone is game for this sort of thing. Not knowing that there is an actual killer in there midst. Which is the thing that has the three of them puzzle on who is the perpetrator. As they didn't put anything past the killer who would do anything to get to the three of them. Even if they have to use Christian as bait to lure them out. Just as the killer did with Jasmine one year ago to get them to follow the breadcrumbs. Until the killer has them right where he or she wants them. For all they know? The killer could of gotten a hold to Christian's cellphone & made it look as if he was the one texting Jill all those messages. Whatever the case maybe? It was a little too late to turn back now? They just have to go along with the flow of things & stay alert to their surrounding. Hoping to not fall for another one of the killers scheme that would effect the outcome of their very survival.

This time around they would have to be extremely careful not to draw attention to themselves. Knowing that there are hidden cameras around the area. Which can expose them in the crowd of people. Where the killer can know their exact location. Which is the strategy the killers is using to pinpoint their position. Which gave Jill the idea that if they stay under the radar the killer would have a problem trying to locate them amongst the crowd. As they took a page out of the killers book to try & blend in with the people. The three of them couldn't help but to feel as if they were being drag into another dangerous situation. As they had a rough time trying to sort out the crowd for Christian. Eventually, they manage to run into Steven who is searching for his sister Kaitlyn. Jill took on the duty to break the bad news to him, as gently as possible. Steven didn't take the news seriously, as he seem humor by it all. Thinking that they are pulling his leg by seeming so serious about it? The three of them felt as if Steven was patronizing them by thinking that this is a game. When in fact it wasn't? The killer would then call Steven's cellphone to stir up more trouble. By manipulating him to believe that everything Jill & Jason's says, is true! Which is sort of like the killer is patronizing him by having him believe that this is all a hoax to get him in the spirit of things.

When in fact, the killer was telling the truth about his sister situation that all boils down to a similar case involving him. That soon he too will feel the wrath of the killers blade. Not knowing better? Steven just decided to play along thinking that this is a joke. He then place his hand over the receiver & whisper to the three of them that this is some good stuff. As he later explain to the three of them the situation. Being that the three of them seem confuse by it all. As he suggested that they should be up for an award for best performance, as a prankster. With a good storyline handed down by the three of them concerning his sister's death. By having one of their friends call him to confirm it. Sort of like a role play? The three had no idea what Steven was babbling about. Considering their role in all of this, in which they denied doing. They then discover that it was the killer Steven is talking too. Jill & Jason knew all so well what the killers is capable of & how manipulative they can be? Jason then ask? "Steven" for his phone so that he can speak with the killer. Things didn't go as plan for Jason when trying to outsmart the killer at his or her own game. As the killer put Jason on the spot by having him think twice about certain issues based on Fact or fiction questions. In result to whether Christian die or not? Would be entirely up to him. Creating a very intense moment by leaving him responsible for his friend life.

The goal was to try & confuse Jason so that he can feel the tremendous pressure of having someone's life in his hands. That his friend life depend on the answers he gives that can play out in either way. In doing so, Jason decided to search the area to see if he could locate Christian. While the killer is focusing on him. He then motion to Jill & Deshawn to let them know what he is doing. While Steven decided to played along by attempting everything they do. In order to see where this thing goes? Steven had no idea what he was getting himself into by not taking the situation seriously. He would soon get the message that this isn't a game. Meanwhile, time was running out for Jason as he try to prolong the conversation to give them more time to find Christian. By avoiding the questions that is given to him by the killer. In which the killer didn't take too likely, given the fact that it is a sign of disrespect to the rules. So instead, the killer made the situation even difficult by putting a time limit on each question. Which didn't leave Jason no other alternative, but to answer the questions within the time limits. Or else he would be held liable for Christian's death by not answering the question in time? Pressure was beginning to build on Jason, as a decision had to be made before the time ran out. Considering that he only had ten seconds to come up with an answer.

The pressure was on! As he attempt to come up with a solution to each of the following questions. Each question he gets correct allows them more time to locate Christian. That had them moving with such urgency. Do to the fact that the questions begin to get harder as time went on. However, there was that one question that seem impossible to answer within the ten second fame. A question that Jason wasn't prepare for? That blindsided him. The thought alone was too significant not to consider as a possibility. Concerning the question that is brought to his attention. Which is to ask him? How sure is he that Christian is still alive. After all! It could of been just a front, to get them in a certain spot to reveal the truth of the fact or fiction conclusion? Based on how he look at certain things that can appear to be misleading. Like the messages that was sent by Christian to Jill's cellphone. As the killer explain to him that he must consider the fact that it was probably "Yours truly"? That made those statements to them? Considering how they would react to certain issues. Containing to their friend's message to notify them that he is in danger. Not knowing the full effect that lies waiting in the midst of things. That led up to this moment in time where he must debate on whether it is fact or fiction. Considering the issue on whether it was Christian or the killers who sent those text messages to Jill's phone?

Time was at the essence as Jason seem surprise by it all that made the situation that much harder to bare. He would soon seek the truth as time begin to expired. Which left him no time to warn the others on what is about to happen. Just as time expire the killer reminded him of his greatest fear of all, before hanging up. Which is the thought of not knowing what to expect to happen. When face with a question mark? On how to prepare for the unexpected. The killer didn't make things easier on Jason, as of what too expect. Now that! Things are getting interesting? Which was the defining moment of the night? When out of nowhere's a hand grab his shoulder. Stunning him! In the process? As he was caught off guard by it all? Despite the fact that he freak out when something simple as making contact seem uncommon. It seem as if the killer succeeded in terrorizing him just from words alone. As it turns out? That his killer was no one other than Christian who suddenly pop up out of the blue. Jason was relieve when he turn around to see that it was Christian who grab him. As it turns out? That it was just a bluff to get him in the spirit of the game. Or as it been told? Christian admit to the text message that he sent to Jill. Only because she sent him one first explaining that his presence is needed. Jill denied the whole thing & try to explain to him that it was the killer who send him those messages which didn't add up.

Do to certain details on how the killer can send text messages from Jill's phone. When her phone has been with her the entire time. Which had them all wondering how can this be possible? Which is one of the million questions that is hidden within the killers secrets. Which is the least of their problems as Steven got another phone call. This time it was from his girlfriend Stacey who is held captive by the killer. The poor girl seem terrified over the phone as they all bare witness the horror that threaten her well being. While, Steven took it as some kind of sick joke to humor him by doing whatever it takes to sucker him in on the prank. According to his belief? Not considering for once that this is a serious matter involving his girlfriend's life. They all try to reason with him to do something based on her horrific cry's for help? Steven had her on speaker phone so that everyone can hear her desperate cry's. It seem as if he was enjoying every minute of it. Not for one second? Thinking that his girlfriend might be in actual danger. Jason had enough! With Steven's lack of concern for his girlfriend's plea for help. As he took it upon himself to take away Steven's phone to see if he can find her, with the help of the others.

Steven would soon follow, as he was infuriated that Jason took his cellphone. As it turns out? That this is all just a game of interest to the killers who wanted nothing more than to see how far they are willing to go? Taking the fact that they don't think of the consequences that may occur in the long run. That they just rush into any situation without giving it any thought what so ever. Which is one of the things the killer pick up on & is using it to lure them in. The sound of Stacey's screams led them away from the crowd to the point where they found themselves deep in the woods. Where Steven would take back his phone & demanded to know what is really going on. So Jill & Jason decided to give him a quick ugly version about what has transpired. Steven was dumbfounded by the news. Do to the fact that he had no idea how serious the situation became. While at the same time finding it hard to believe that this is really happening. Which seems kind of skeptical to him do to how it pertains to his involvement in all of this? Yet alone the involvement of his sister & girlfriend for that matter. At that point? The screaming had suddenly stop! Almost as if she was being gag by the killer to end the suspense. Knowing that Jason & the others are nearby? The killer prepare for the surprise of a life time that would leave them at a crossroads.

CHAPTER 16

Facing The Truth

Somehow they manage to find Stacey, who is tie to a tree with no sign of the killer in site. Unable to speak? Stacey begin to mumble to try & warn them of the danger that awaits them. Not acknowledging her forewarning that something terrible is about to take place. They manage to get to her very quickly, while obsering the area for anything suspicious. Steven & Jason went to work on releasing Stacey from her restraints, while the others was on the lookout. Within that one second Jill & the others got destracted for a moment. When Jason took the rag off her mouth to get a better understanding of what she was trying to said. Which was to lookout! That gave the killer the little time needed to arrange an attack on a unsuspected person. Which seem to be Christian who was caught off guard by the killer sudden appearance. That no one seen it coming except for Stacey who try to warn them. Which put them all in a awkward position, as the killer in the slicker was ready to claim Christian's life with the hook he or she had as a weapon. Just as all seem lost of trying to save Christian from the killer's wrath? Out came a mischievous laugh from Stacey who yell out the word "Gotcha"? It seem as if Jason & the others couldn't catch a break from all of the nonsense that is taking place.

That they were a little fed up with all of the B.S of being a pawn in other people's pranks. As the killer once again made a fool of them by torturing their minds emotionally. What better way than to make them out as a joke. Which seems to be the case according to Steven. Who was starting to believe the hype that there was an actual killer in the area. He sort of wanted to kick himself for allowing Jason & Jill to brainwash him. By having him believe that Stacey was in serious danger & that his sister is dead. It was useless to try & convince him that this is what the killer wanted him to think. In order to keep them from seeing the truth behind what is really going on. Which reminded Christian, Jill & Jason of the smoking mirrors that plays a huge part in tonight's event. Not a second sooner! Another killer made a unexpected appearance by slipping in on them undetected. While wearing the masked of torment, which represents one of the three Faces of Death masks. The killer would target Deshawn since he was the closest one. Which left him vulnerable to the killer's sudden attack. The killer seem to catch everyone off guard by the rare appearance. Stabbing Deshawn multiple of times in the chest. Before realizing that it was just a false alarm.

Which almost ended up in turmoil, as the person in the mask was inches away from being beaten to death. As it turns out, that the person in the mask was a close friend of Steven. Who reveal himself as Kaitlyn's boyfriend. Who has been looking for her everywhere's, but doesn't have a clue on where she must of run off too. Steven jokingly, "announce that she is dead" according to the others? Which seems like one big joke to them. That infuriated Jason do to the fact that the two of them is playing with his emotions. Which in fact upseted the rest of them as well, that led to an argument between them. Stacey try to defuse the situation by stepping in between them. As Steven had enough & decided to step away for a second to relieve himself. The argument would continue between them, that is? Until, Stacey made an important discovery? Based on someone, who is claiming to be something their are not. As she discovers her friend Kyle lying yards away in the bushes dead. She didn't know if it was really him or not. Do to the fact that he had a mask on his face. The others had a hard time understanding the point she was trying to make. Stacey simply express to them that she thought that it was Kyle in the slicker outfit the whole while they were pranking them.

They would soon reveal the truth as Stacey remove the mask & realize that it was indeed Kyle lying there dead as a doornail. Which brought up the question? That if it wasn't Kyle in the "Slicker" than who was it? As they all notices that the person in the slicker didn't reveal him or herself, once the joke was over. Which led them to believe that everything that has happen so far involving Stacey was real. Eventually, they got the message & realize that someone was missing. As it turns out that the missing person was Steven who went to take a leak in the bushes & has yet to return. The same could be said, about the killer in the slicker who also disappear from site along with Steven.

Desperation suddenly kick in as they realize that Steven is in great danger. The fact of the matter is that he has no idea that the person in the slicker is the killer. They search high & low for Steven deep in the woods. Come to find out that they were a little too late. As they all discover Steven's body lying face down in the dirt. At first they didn't know what to make of it? On whether this is some sort of joke or not? They would soon find out that this was no joke. As Jason turn over the body & realize that Steven had suffer from a deep gash on his neck from the hook use by the killer. This sort of thing terrorize Stacey & Roger "Kaitlyn's boyfriend". To the point, where they both seem traumatize. Do to fact that they wasn't mentally prepare for what they just witness.

Stacey seem terrified by it all? As Jill & Jason try to fill the two of them in on what is going on? Stacey couldn't bare the thought of being watch under close supervision by the killers who has eyes everywhere's around the camp site. The thought alone was too much for Stacey to handle. Which led to her departure from the group. As she ran wildly through the woods to escape from the nightmare that haunts her. Follow by the footsteps of Roger who took off behind her. In order to get her back within the group before it was too late. Roger stood on her trail the deeper they went into the woods. Finally! He manage to catch up with her, as they both fell to the ground. They both were exhausted from the long run. Which puts the two of them in an awkward position. As Roger try to calm her down. Do to the fact that she seems beside herself. Which led to his own down fall of failing to understand what's at stake. By risking his life. As the killer was in place to claim Roger as the next victim. Which is unexpected? For Roger who was unaware of the killer's presence at the time. The killer took full advantage of the opportunity that was giving. By killing him with the hook use as a potential weapon the moment he turn around. Splattering blood all over Stacey who seem shaking up by the gruesome site. As the killer suddenly turn his or her attention toward Stacey who realize that she's next on the killer's list.

Somehow, she manage the strength to get to her feet & take off running. With the killer right behind her moving at a rapid pace, as she attempts to get away. Stacey had no idea what direction she was going. Do to the fact that she seem lost. She was hoping to get someone's attention by yelling for help. Then suddenly! she found herself alone lost in the dark with no sign of the killer anywhere's. Thinking to herself that the killer must have duck off in the woods. That left her wondering what is the killer's next move. Leaving her with the mindset that she is being watch closely by a certain individual that is driven by the smell of fear. Which made her situation that much difficult to deal with, knowing what she knows. Which makes all the differents pertaining to the levels of fear. That constantly ran through her mind about the uncertainty. Feeling as if though, she is being prey upon, in this endless cycle of a game. Stacey would soon get the surprise of her life when she turn around & came face to face with Lisa who scare the living daylights out of her. Stun by the encounter with Lisa turn out to be a sudden rush of absolute fear. Something that she wasn't prepare for in the least, despite the fact that she seem out of it. The poor girl didn't know what to think as she seem frighten of everyone.

Which includes Alan & Jerry as well. Who wasn't that far behind Lisa. Stacey was emotionally wreck by what she had witness two minutes ago. Lisa try her best to comforter Stacey. While Alan & Jerry search the area for the killer who seem to disappear from site. Not long after? Alan receive a texts from Jason who suggested that they return to the cabin immediately. They all rush back to the cabin quickly to regroup. Once they all met up at the cabin. It was then that they realize that the two police officers they spoke too earlier. Was nothing more than a imposter making light of the situation. Which points out the obvious that their badge & uniform was just a costume for the party. Which had them all thinking about how they could of miss not seeing past the get-up. However, Jill & the others couldn't help but to notices all the blood on Stacey's clothes. As they kind of summarize what may have happen? When she took off running in the woods. Follow by Roger who didn't make it back, which kind of speechs for itself. Knowing their situation & how it affect's them. Christian decided to get a hold to the real police by calling the emergency line. Which seem impossible to do, according to the area they are in?

Being that he or anyone else for that matter. Couldn't get a signal. Do to all of the trees & landscape in a deserted area. Which made it hard to make a call outside the region. It was made clear that the only calls they can make is within their location. Which limited their options on what is the best thing to do, right now? Which led to another idea from Deshawn who suggested that they could always drive down to the police station in one of the cars. What a splendid idea to come up with as they decided on who will stay & who will go. Jason decided to stay with his crew & the two girls. While Christian, Deshawn & Stacey go for help. That way? Stacey could relieve some stress by talking with the police. That the ride would be good for her. Not wasting anymore time on the matter.

The three went on their mission to get a hold to the police. Which means that they would have to re-enter the crowd to get to the car. Hoping to avoid the killers at all cost. Somehow, they manage to get to Christian's car without any hassle from the killers. Which seems kind of odd, considering that the killer has them in sight. Thanks to the hidden camera's surrounding the area.

It seem as if they ran into more trouble once they got to the car. It looks as if someone busted out the windows & flated the tires to his car. Also leaving a message that states the obvious that someone from their camp is with-holding a secret. That is spray painted on the hood of his car. With one of the faces of death mask lying on the front seat. Which led Christian to turn to Jill & Jason vehicles. Which was also broken into? With the same result that says "I know your secret". That was painted on the hood of the two cars as well. Each car had a mask in it, that was place in the front seat. Which was reveal? As the other two faces of death masks. That set Stacey off when she notice that something wasn't right. Christian & Deshawn begin to get frustrated with Stacey. As she begin to have flashbacks as reality started to kick in once again. She then begin to get beside herself, as they both try to calm her down. Do to the fact that she is making a scene, which attract's unwanted guests. Which led them to a random vehicle, in which they try to break into, do to the circumstances. That led to the alarm going off, which puts them on the spot. To the point where they got some unwanted attention from certain individuals. Who seem concern about what is going on.

CHAPTER 17

Cruel Intentions

Which started to draw in a crowd of people, do to all of the madness that is taking place. Between the alarm going off & Stacey on the verge of a meltdown. Cause a huge scene to the public. The three of them started to notices people from the crowd pointing at them, while looking down at their phones. Almost as if they are being display to the public by something of interest that capture many viewers. The three didn't know what to make of it, as they seem confuse on the subject. As one good samaritan came down to the car to fill them in. On why everyone seem amuse about their situation. As it turns out that the joke was on them, as part of a game call "Gotcha"! It seem as if someone had the audacity to upload a video containing tonight's event. By breaking down the physics of how fearful the videos are of them. Given their worse scenario. By the killers who is making a mockery of them. Who is enlighten by the crowd's reaction. That the killers is using to spread the message throughout the crowd to encourage them all. By rallying the troops in order to keep this thing going. Chaos ensues, as the crowd seem amuse by the videos & wanted to duplicate what they seen.

At this point the situation became grim for the three of them of not knowing their predicament enlight of all this madness. Do to the fact that now? They are in deeply over their heads. It seem kind of crazy, but the best thing for them to do now. Is to head back to the cabin to warn the others about the difficulties they are left to face? The thing is? That they would have too face their fears in all this commotion that surrounding them. Only because they were left in a peculiar position by the killers. Who put them all on display. Leaving the three of them to fend for themselves from a hostile crowd. Who seem amuse on what they saw on video that entitle them to demonstrate the reenactment from the video clips. The three of them couldn't help but to notices all of the attention they was getting from the crowd. As they could almost feel the many of eyes watching them. As they move along? However, there was one individual who caught the attention of Stacey. A person dress in a hideous goblin costume. In fact, it was the same person that grab a hold to Jason early on. Again, this person in the goblin costume seems to be acting very oddly. By toying around with Stacey to the point where. This individual would ducking in & out of site each time she try to point out the pursuiter to Deshawn & Christian.

Who they didn't come across according to her description of a person in a goblin costume. Which made the two of them think that maybe she is delusional. Thinking that the poor girl had finally crack from the pressure. That had her convince that she was seeing things that isn't really there? That led Stacey to question herself on the subject. On how Deshawn & Christian are not seeing what she see. Which led her to believe that maybe she has lost it? Which seems impossible! According to her eyes that is undeniable to the truth. That every which way she turns, she see the mask of the goblin. At that moment in time, Stacey became fed up with everything & became disoriented. As she ran wildly through the crowd yelling to everyone that someone is after her? Christian & Deshawn attempted to go after her, but fail to do so? As they lost site of her within the large crowd of people. In the midst of things, Stacey than realize that she made the wrong decision by running away. Instead of showing compassion of concern for her, the crowd got intensify? As they encourage this sort of thing. As they took on the role of the killer. Not knowing that there will be consequences for this sort of action. Stacey knew that now she was in deep trouble. As she couldn't make heads or tails on who amongst the crowd is the killer.

As they all made the attempt to come after her since she made herself out as the victim. She then found herself surrounded by all sorts of people wearing scary costumes. The scary thing about it, was that she knew the killer was somewhere's close by watching. Just waiting for the opportunity to present itself. Her only chance was to high tail it out of there before she end up dead. That led her deep in the woods to get away from the crowd who is in full pursuit. Somehow, she manage to duck away from them all by hiding inside an old shabby broke down pickup truck. That kept Stacey safe from the hunters that is in search for her. She could hear them as they past by the truck. Making a mockery of her by toying around with her mind. By making it out as some sort of game. Stacey was so sure that someone would find her inside of the truck. The question was? Who would that person be? That made things that much complicated to deal with. Then suddenly! There was silence, as everything seems to calm down a bit. Which led Stacey to believe that the people that was after her, had come & gone. As she slowly lift up her head to take a look around the area to see if they really left. Halfway up to the viewing point, she was stunned!

By a black cat who hop onto the hood of the truck. That blindsided her. As a result? Scaring her half to death by expecting the worse at that fine moment. Stacey show a sign of relief once she notices that it was just a cat. However, she seen her chance to get away. Not feeling as if the truck is a liable place to hide. Fearing that they will come back to this area & that someone is bound to find her there. Stacey than ease her way from the truck & made a break for it. Although, it felt as if she still had the mindset that the killer was still around waiting & watching, in the distance. She then begin to freak out, as she try to find her way out. All of the spooky sounds & noises of the woods didn't make things any easier containing to her situation. At that point? She started to hear someone crying out for help in the far distance. Figuring that someone was in danger? Stacey begin to follow the desperate cry's to see if she can assist that person. She also try calling out to whoever it is out there to try & pinpoint the victim's location. Which eventually led her to the ramp by the lake. By then, the cry's for help stop! The instant Stacey reach the point where she thought the sounds of cry's was coming from?

Figuring that she arrive too late, Stacey begin searching the area. While constantly calling out to the individual in order to save that person. Strangely she got no responds, which led her right in the hands of the killer who now has her in plain sight. As the thought ran through her mind constantly about how the killer manipulated her by a little game called "Gotcha"? At that moment, Stacey begin to experience the meaning of fear. As she begin to have that unpleasant feeling that she is being watch. She had no idea what to expect to happen. Now that the killer has set his or her sights on her. Which makes things a bit scarier for her. Do to the issue that she is unprepared for what is about to take place. She just knew that something bad was about to happen by the way things unfold. Just as things seem at it's worse! A bit of relief came over Stacey as she heard the voice of that certain someone again. This time! it seems as if the voice was coming from underneath the ramp. Stacey then made her way to the end of the ramp. Where she got down on all fours & bent over the edge of the ramp to see who is under there? Just as she was at the verge of seeing what is going on? A hand! Reach in & grab the back of her head & push it down into the water.

It was the killer who suddenly appear out of nowhere's dress in the attire from the movie Urban Legend. Who made it difficult for Stacey who struggle the whole time she was held under water. Who I might add? Die in a very violent manner that resulted to her drowning. The killer would then push Stacey's lifeless body into the lake where it would drift off into the distance. Meanwhile, back at Jason's cabin it seems as if Deshawn & Christian made it back alright. However, the two couldn't help but to notices that some of the group is missing. The fact that Alan & Jerry was M.I.A puts the two of them in great danger. As Christian & Deshawn try to explain to the rest of them about the danger headed their way. About the issues concerning the cameras that is being use to exploit them all to the crowd. Who acknowledge this sort of behavior. Not long before than, Alan & Jerry had made their way back to the cabin. They both seem exhausted as if they had been running from someone or something. Alan & Jerry both needed a moment to catch their breath before explaining what went on with the two of them. The two of them seem surprise by the reaction they got from the crowd. As they explain to the others that eveyone seems to be acting as if they are the killers.

By imitating what seems to be the logical response to something this horrific. By all means? Having no idea the horror that is conceal amongst them. As they all was deceive by what they saw, which is blinding them from seeing the truth. As Christian made the point that everyone amongst the crowd is now a threat to them. Considering the fact that everyone has join in on the game. That plays a part in the thick of things to come, which is a scam for the ages? Which had them all wishing that they shouldn't have come. As Jill came to terms that the only reason she decided to take part in this gathering. Was because of the e-mail she receive from Jason. In which he denied doing & claim that Jill was the one who sent him an e-mail on the subject. That led Christian to believe that it was the two of them that sent him an e-mail about the whole getting together thing. Which had the three of them confuse on the matter about who sent out the e-mails, if it wasn't none of them. Which is a question in itself? The only explanation that seem reasonable is that somehow the killer got a hold to their personal information & use it as a way to get the three of them together again.

Which still didn't add up on why the killer insist on getting them together. When in fact the killers could of seek the three of them out, one by one?

Which to them seem like the better option, considering the fact that they wouldn't expect it. Which left the three of them questionable on the matter. Almost as if things didn't make any sense, what so ever. By having the three of them come all this way to conclude that someone is withholding a secret. A secret that may involve each one of them "Perhaps"? Things became intense for Jason as he demanded to know what the secret is? He became highly upset about this whole ordeal that somebody knows! Something about someone in general? That had them all wondering about one another that the killer speaks of? This was a defining moment for them all as they try to make light of the situation. Taking that no one would step up & reveal the truth by putting things in perspective. Which had each of them suspicious of one another. Containing to the secret that is being upheld. A secret that may shed some light on this entire case. That led Jason to question Deshawn on the picture of him & Amanda with Thomas & Jasmine. That was sent to them all from a suposedly friend? Deshawn would go on to say that he & Thomas were childhood friends & that the picture was from springbreak of last year. What Jill, Jason & Christian didn't know was that Jasmine & Thomas was dating around that time. That soon they would break up not long afterwards.

CHAPTER 18

The Ultimate Deception

*Deshawn would also go as far as to acknowledge the fact that Thomas &
Jasmine are not the killers. He believe's that the two are being use as part of the
scheme to enhance the thrill of the game that is being displayed by the killers.
That traces back to the two of them, which puts the blame on them. Do to their
history together, which cause for some concern. Being that Thomas & Jasmine
had suddenly turn up missing when things was at it's peak. Also the fact that
Thomas was a close friend of theirs? Who probably knows a secret about one of
them. Who I might add? Is using this personal information to torment them.
Which was one way of looking at it? From Jason stand point of view, according
to how things unfolded. On the other hand Jill & Christian didn't know
what to believe at this point. Lisa made the assumption that maybe Deshawn
has a point. Which led her to believe that the killer is trying to frame them.
Even though, the two has already met their demise. Which caught everyone's
attention on the subject that led to a debate about the situation involving
Thomas & Jasmine's existence. The fact that Jill & Jason wanted to know how
in the world Lisa would suggest such a thing. Without any knowledge on who
Thomas & Jasmine were as far as how they are perceive by her.*

*As Christian pointed out to Lisa that he didn't recall discussing the incident
involving Thomas & Jasmine with her at all? The only thing that was mention
to her the other night was the situation involving himself, Jason & Jill on that
horrifying night of halloween past. He too seem curious on how she came across
this information. Lisa seem surprise by all of the questions being thrown that
her from every angle. Almost as if she was the one being interrogated? Lisa try
to explain to them about the facts that was presented to her that made her come*

to this conclusion? Which makes all the sense in the world according to Alan & Jerry who sided with Lisa on the matter. However, just as things begin to become clear that there was no secrets being held between them. In comes a huge surprise that would say otherwise? When Deshawn spotted a hand held voice recorder lying on the shelf above the fireplace. Which looks as if it was hidden away by someone "In Particular"! As he told everyone to get a load of this? Once Lisa got a real good look at what was shown to them. She begin making a scene by expressing her legal rights. By claiming that the voice recorder belongs to her & that there are some confidential things that she whether not bring up.

As she ask them? To respect her privacy. Which seems kind of weird considering how she is behaving over this voice recorder. That had the four of them believing that she is hiding something from them. Not including Alan & Jerry who were seen looking at one another with a concern look on their faces. As Lisa demanded that Deshawn hand over what belongs to her. That led him to question her about the tape. As he wanted to know along with everyone else? What is so important that she doesn't want anyone to know. That has her behaving this way? Which led them to believe that they stumble onto something. Which struck a nerve? Considering how cool Lisa remain through all of this chaos. To avoid any further confrontation between them? Alan suggested that they just give her what she wants to keep down confusion. Which didn't set well with Jill, Jason & Christian who wanted to know what is on the tape that is so sacred to her. They would soon reveal the secrets behind the message that was left on the tape. A message that expose Lisa's secret for who she really is? In reference to her being the killer, along with Alan & Jerry as her accomplice. Who voices were also on the tape. Explaining in plain details the conversation between the three of them. Concerning the killing spree that is being display on camera by the three of them. Considering how they are seeking to do whatever it takes to hunt them down one by one?

That eventually led up to the point of view? Which is for them to take note that Alan, Jerry & Lisa "Knows"! Refering to their predicament that places Jill & her friends on the radar. By getting information on them all & using it against them. By capturing it all on camera as a way of seeking out their worse fears. With the note Deshawn claims Lisa left for him the other night. Explaining how they should scare Jill, Jason & Christian by playing a prank on them. Which is the ultimate deception as things begin to become clear to Jill & the others. The fact that Lisa had been studying them all along? By using the information given to her by Christian as a stepping stone to acquire the knowledge needed to pull this thing off. The voice recorder had also mention how they should remain undetected if their plan is going to work. Lisa denied the allegations that was brought up on the tape. Claiming that someone had tampered with the tape? As Lisa try stressing to them that the killer edited out certain details of what was really said? However, she did admitted that it was them on the tape, but it was the killer who twisted their words around. By making it seems as if they are the one's doing the killing. Jason & the others wasn't at all convince by the story & demanded the truth. The three of them try to reframe from revealing the truth to them. Which made Jason angry with them do to the fact that they were avoiding the questions.

Jason became infuriated with them beating around the bush, as he was at the end of his rope. Which led to him getting violent with Jerry & Alan about the secret they refuse to reveal. Christian at that point grab a hold of Jason to try & calm him down. In the sense? Christian can understand Jason's pain of feeling betrayed by his two closes friends. At this point? The three of them didn't feel it was necessary to keep quiet when there is so much at stake. As Lisa decided to break her silence & reveal to them the truth. She begin by telling them that she is an undercover reporter for the local news. Who is accompany by Alan & Jerry as her cameramen. She then explain to them about their assignment which is to unmask the notorious serial killers. Which explains all of the hidden camera's around the campsite. She then would go on to mention that they had been working on this case since the first onslaught of deaths that paralyze the city with fear. Which led her to the three of them who survive the incident involving last year's massacre. The approach was to get close to the three of them. So that they can get the moral of the story. Which is the defining moment in their investigation to piece together the evidence needed to solve this thing.

Lisa wanted to get more insight from each one of them about their predicament containing to last year's halloween massacre. By befriending them? That led Alan & Jerry to team up with Jason who wanted nothing more than to solve this thing. Just as bad as they wanted too? While Lisa stood in touch with Christian the whole time. As she reveal another secret to them. As it turns out? That it was Lisa, claiming to be Abigail? His long awaited mystery girl who chatted with him online. She simply explain to him that Abigail was her code name on the website. So that her cover wouldn't be blown? As she reminded *them that they never once, use their full names. Which entitle them to use a false profile to remain conceal from the killers. Who somehow figure out their secret & has use that secret against them. Which had Jill concern about all of the secrecy that is going on? As she pointed out the obvious about her situation involving a secret admirer. Out of curiosity? Jill wanted to know if it was Lisa who was the mystery person behind the scenes that try to get her attention. By spreading the message with certain facts, in order for Jill to get the memo.*

Lisa acknowledge being the secret admirer that had been studying her for quite sometime. Although, she denied having anything to do with leading Jill on? With having her to believe that there's an actual admirer. As Lisa pointed out that whoever this other secret admirer is? Maybe a stalker who intentions is to sabotage her. Which brought their attention to that certain someone. Who loves playing this sort of game? Which so happens to be the notorious masked killers. Who's identities is unknown? Which can be also said, about Jill's Secret admirer that seems to have a connection with her. That plays a huge part in regards to how it relates too Lisa. Based on the similarities concerning to how they both were secret admirer's of Jill? It seem as Jason & Christian was approach in the same way by the three of them. By admiring both Christian & Jason, only to be deceive by a lie. In order for Lisa & her gang to take the necessary steps to get what they want. Even if it's at a cost? Which didn't set well with Jill and her friends, do to the fact that Lisa & her crew use them. Lisa simply explain that this was necessary. Based on the fact that it is the nature of their business. Which had to be done considering how they are the center piece of this investigation? Which is why Lisa sent Jill a laptop, along with the cellphone. Do to the fact that it was her only way to keep taps on Jiil. Considering that she was busy trying to get close to Christian. While Alan & Jerry were assign as Jason's film crew. In order to investigate the halloween murders. Which was the goal they were pushing for? Which led Lisa to believe that by keeping taps on the three of them. Will led them to the killers? Lisa simply came up with a solution that suddenly dawned on her. That the person claiming to be Jill's secret admirer is no one other than the killer.

Who also kept tabs on the three of them as well. Which led Lisa to believe that it's someone close to them. Who has been studying each one of them closely. Which explains the mystery concerning the e-mails that was sent to each of them about the reunion. That it was the killer all along setting up the stage to reenact the horror that haunted them for so long. Only to pick up where they left off one year ago. Christian ask' Lisa? Was there anyone in particular who they believe is the killer. That they should have some insight on what is going on around them. Considering all of the cameras they have in place. Lisa & her crew had no leads on who it maybe considering the fact that they too had been exposed. However, there was one individual in particular that they had their sites on? That stood out from the rest. That being the person in the hideous goblin costume who seem kind of strange looking. In which they all briefly encounter the mysterious stranger. As they all admitted that there is something very peculiar about this person. As they all took a plague to unmask this person before the night is over.

CHAPTER 19

The Mystery Unfolds

They figure that the person behind the goblin mask holds the key to all the secrets. If only they could seek out that certain someone within the large crowd of people. Which seems impossible? According to how the killers seem to blend in with the crowd by constantly changing their appearance with all sorts of different attire. Which reminded them that there is another killer lurking around the area besides the one they lay eyes on. At that moment, they felt as if they were at a disadvantage. Do to the fact that they had no intellect on why this is happening to them? That had them all discussing the matter, in which it pertains to them. As they try to make sense of it? Lisa had mention to them that maybe she can shed some light on certain issues. Refering to the Faces of Death masks. In which, she begin explaining the history behind the agenda masks. Lisa stated that the three masks is fairly known for it's comparison to each it's own. In regards to how the three masks reflects it's image according to the symbols. The symbols that simulate Fear, Torment & Pain. As a way of expressing the different types of death's. A legendary folktale that has to deal with vengeance. According to Urban Legend tales! The moral of the story is that the tribe clan would use the masks to seek revenge against those who opposed them.

That the tribe would display each of the masks description in order to state it's true concept of retribution. Which plays in the hands of the killers who is using famous slashers from the movies as a way to evaluate the definition behind each of the three masks description. In which it is refer to as (The Urban Killers of Legend). Which is the concept that surrounds this entire story. According to Lisa's intuition? Christian & the others seem shock by Lisa story in reference to the secrets behind the Faces of Death masks. Alan & Jerry replied that Lisa is a real pro at what she does? Which brings out the best in them, as her cameramen. As the two would go on to mention that this is the sort of work they do? In order to seek the truth behind every unsolved mystery that go's unnoticed. Jerry simply explain the situation to them that when the police has a difficult time solving a case. The three of them would step in & take over the investigation. Lisa refer to the operations as a huge success whenever they are call upon. That this case? For some reason, is the most difficult task they had to put up with, on every level. Words alone doesn't describe how ironic this one case has become. Having to deal with confusion, conflict & uncertainty all at once. With that said? Lisa & her crew remain focus on the task at hand without any signs of despair on letting up.

That somehow they were going to reveal the truth behind the killings & it's connection to the killers. Which is originally based on the action's of Eric Johnson & his involvement in this investigation. As Lisa explain to them that she was schedule to interview Eric the night before he escape the Mental Institution for a second time. To give his statement on what happened that night the Hatchet Family was killed along with some of the students attending the party that halloween night. Since than she has been hearing all sorts of rumors about Eric. Concerning the murders that traces back to him & another who remains unknown to this day. Jason decided to clear the air by setting the record straight. By strongly suggesting that Eric had been frame for those murders. The same way the killers has try to frame each one of them. By trying to manipulate them into believing that there's a traitor amongst them. Who seems guilty in the eyes of the killers who "Knows a Secret"? Jill & Christian simply explain Eric's situation, concerning to his confessions about his role in all of this? Which was mention to them at the Galleria Hall of last year's halloween disaster. Jill couldn't stress enough of what it would mean if Lisa could clear the air by doing a story on Eric concerning to his innocents.

Lisa on the other hand knew of the circumstances that has prevented her from doing a story on him? Do to the fact that there is so much evidence pin against him. Which led her to believe that there is more to the story than what Eric is letting on? Which is why Lisa is good at what she does? By letting them know once again? As a reminder! That it was her job to uncover the truth. By all means necessary? The decision was then made that someone would accompany Lisa to her van. Where all of the setup is located. To see if she *can come up with a solution by searching for any kind of clue. That would shed some light on who is behind these killings. Deshawn decided that he would assist Lisa on the walk to her van. While the others stayed behind, as a precaution. Do to the fact that they had two walkie talkie between them. In which, Lisa took one of them, so that Alan & Jerry could walk her through the controls. Of obtaining the live feed from the cameras remaining. In hopes of revealing something worthwhile. With everything in place the two took off into the woods. Making their way toward the van. Which wasn't very far from the camp site. In fact, it was hidden away deep in the bushes. Where it would be impossible to spot. It seems as if Lisa & Deshawn made it to the van okay without any unexpected surprises.*

However, once they step inside of the van to begin searching for answers. They notices that the setup was all wrong? Almost as if the equipment had been fiddle with? Which wasn't a big deal, thinking that maybe it was Alan or Jerry who is responsible for the mix up. The problem was an easy fix as Lisa would simply radio in Alan or Jerry to walk her through the process. It wasn't long before than as all of the data base was uploaded to the computer. Setting up the surveillance video to all of the remaining cameras surrounding the area. Things were going smooth up until the cameras begin to show footage of their friends being killed in a playback video. Not to metion the video of the two of them leaving the cabin a couple of minutes ago, headed toward the news van. As they were the one's being under surveillance by the killer who flip the script on them. By using Lisa's own cameras against her. At that point, Lisa & Deshawn felt uneasily. Do to the fact that they were being watch. The two didn't waste any time at all with trying to move as quickly as possible to get back to the cabin. They both try to get in touch with Alan & Jerry to warn them all about what has surface. It seems as though they had a rough time trying to get through to them. Do to the fact that there was a lot of static on the walkie talkie. As they couldn't make out what was being said on the other end of the device?

Deshawn became fed up with everything that has gone down. As he begin to show intolerance of not being able to withstand anymore of the foolishness that is being display. As he decided to take matters into his on hands by seeking out the vicious murderer. Even it he have to unmask everyone at the party. By having to use any means to find the one responsible? As he told Lisa, that there is only one way to handle this problem. He then reveal to her the one thing that is going to put an end to all of this? At that point? Deshawn pull out a gun. *Thinking that this is the solution to their problems. Which was a dumb move on his part, knowing that he is under surveillance. It wasn't long before than that the two of them were spotted by the crowd. Who seem pretty anxious to feed off the fear of others. Which is now the stipulation of the game even though, it was just for fun to some. A joke that Lisa & Deshawn didn't want no part of? While it may seem like fun to others. There were certain individuals who seize the moment to take full advantage of the opportunity given to them. By using the crowd as cover to remain hidden from the two of them. Lisa knew that they would have to stay as far away from the crowd as possible. To avoid the killers who is waiting amongst the crowd for them. The two of them would have to come up with a plan soon? To avoid being caught up in the middle of the mayhem.*

As the two of them stare danger in the face with the many scary costumes that threw them off. Of trying to sort out the perpetrators amongst the large amount of people. Waiting to create some turmoil. The two then begin to back track their steps. By slowly stepping away from the rough patch, which seems to be the crowd. The crowd would then erupt when Deshawn accidentally step on a twig. Which set them off? Creating all sort of turmoil within the crowd. Leaving Lisa & Deshawn in the center of the mayhem. Their only chance of escape was to fire a shot in the air. That led everyone to scatter the area. Which was the worse thing Deshawn could of done. By doing this? He & Lisa got bum rush? Which separated them from one another. If that wasn't bad enough, just think about the consequences he now faces. The fact that he lost the gun in the process & was unable to retrieve it? At that point, Deshawn begin getting stab from every angle. Not knowing who it is? That is doing the stabbing. Considering the fact that he was surrounded by all sort of people wearing scary masks. Who is trying to get away? Which is a crucial moment for Deshawn of not knowing what direction the assault is coming from? A mistake that cost him dearly that resulted to his own down fall. That ends with him dying.

Lisa however, made it back to the cabin safely, even though she bearly escape being trample to death by the crowd. Jill seem concern about Deshawn who didn't make it back. Lisa simply told her to not worry because Deshawn was fully capable of looking after himself. That soon or later he is going to show up within the matter of minutes. In the meanwhile, Lisa had suggested that maybe they should dispose all of the remaining cameras surrounding the area. As she explain to them all the reason why they should pull the plug on

*this investigation. That all the while Lisa & her crew was studying Jill &
the others. The killers had been studying them in the process? Making things
all so difficult to uncover the truth behind the shattered glass that crumble
right before their eyes. In hopes of revealing the mystery that back fire onto
the three of them. Lisa & her crew must now cover their tracks in order to
remain undetected from prying eyes in the area. It is a must that they do this?
In order for them to stay anonymous, even though, the killers knows their
secret. Which leave them no other alternative, in reference to them going back
into the danger zone to retrieve their equipment. Before their cover is blown.*

*The plan was to destroy any evidence that would link the three of them to
this case. Which would destroy their reputation if the people knew what they
were doing. That all of their hard work would be in vain. They all decided to
split up into groups in order to stand a better chance against the killers who is
on the prowl. The decision was made that Jason & Jerry would tag along with
Lisa to remove the remaining cameras. Since she is the one who knows where
they are? Considering the fact that Lisa was the one who set up the cameras.
The night before, around the camp site when the others was asleep. Jill on
the other hand would stay at the cabin to wait for the arrival of her friend
Deshawn. While Christian & Alan would head for the news van to retrieve
any & all data concerning to this case. Before leaving Jerry handed over the
walkie talkie to Christian just in case they get in touch with Deshawn. Which
was to let him know that Jill is waiting on him back at the cabin. Little did
they know? That Deshawn is now accountable for. As one of the many death's
in the recent murders surrounding tonight's event. Without any knowledge of
his death, they all exceeded to go on as plan.*

CHAPTER 20

Disguising The Truth

With the plan in full swing, they gather the information needed to put an end to this conspiracy. As Christian & Alan retrieve what was needed to clear the air. By cleaning up the mess that was left? Containing to Lisa's involvement as a undercover news reporter. In which, she wanted to remain that way too keep things in perspective. However, as they were leaving the news van to head back to the cabin. They started to hear sounds from the walkie talkie. Almost as if someone was trying to contact them from the other end. Christian try repeatedly to get through to Deshawn, but what he got was something far more worse. To his surprise! It was the killer who responded to his call. Which was unexpected? Considering how things unfolded that led Christian to spill the beans on what they were doing. By mistakenly taking the killer for Deshawn. Which is a mistake that is going to have some implications in the long run. Which plays in the hands of the killer who announce the stipulations to a game called "I Spy"? A game where the killers would spy on a certain individual who is unaware of their presence. As the killer explain in plain details how it was their job to find which one of their friends is the next target. The moral of the game is to try & identify which of the three people dress in the Faces of Death costumes is the killer. Depending on how they are perceived on the cameras?

Which makes it that much difficult to withstand the pressure of locating three individuals who may or may not be the killers. Which is a real test considering how would they measure up to the challenge. That the answer they seek may come to a surprise to them all, of uncovering the truth. As the killer left them with these final words? Which is "Just what is their greatest fear of all"? Which comes to no surprise, as they got a little taste of what's to come. By showing video clips of them all in their current positions. As the killers took certain steps by tracking down each one of them. The question was? Which of them the killers has their sites on. Alan & Christian had a choice to make concerning who is in danger here? Whether it was Jill who is all alone at the cabin or Lisa & the gang who is out removing the cameras amongst the crowd. Not for one second thinking about themselves who is also included in the mix. The only difference is that they knew what was going to happen & the others didn't. That led Christian to believe that it was Jill who was the one in danger. Which makes perfect sense do to the fact that she is all alone at the cabin waiting for Deshawn to show up. The two of them cautiously made their way back to the cabin to warn Jill about the danger ahead.

They return to the cabin to find out that there was no sign of Jill anywhere's? As they search all around the camp site for her. Leaving an unpleasant feeling, as if though something is wrong about this entire situation. The fact that this entire set up seems a bit unusual for their taste. Almost as if they were being drag into some kind of plot that would test their insight on what to make out from all of this? A lesson that states the obvious when it comes down to knowing who their real enemies are? Of what purpose is attended for such aggression being displayed by the killers. In order to get their point across by setting the record straight. According to Alan's theory that there is more to this story that meets thee eye. The fact that vengeance plays a huge role in these events. The fact that they miss something along the way. While investing all of their time & energy into this case. Which led Alan to believe that this is what the killers wanted. To showcase these killings in order for them to get the message that this is not some random killing? That there are reasons behind these killings, which seems to be personal. That the secret the killers were refering too, had to deal with guilt? Which is the concept of this entire game. Which is to scout out the guilty party by displaying them for who they really are.

As things begun to become clear to them. Only to realize the danger that is going to surface within the matter of minutes. That now places them all in danger. The bad thing about this whole ordeal is that their friends has no idea what is about to transpire. They had no idea what to make about Jill's situation based on her sudden disappearance. The two of them risk their own lives by searching the crowd to find the others. While searching through the crowd it seems as if their minds were playing tricks on them. It just so happens that there seems to be some confusion. On whether they were being misled by *a duplicate costume that resembles the Faces of Death attire. Which is hard to tell the differents between what is real. The fact that they are surrounded by all sorts of scary costumes, which kind of plays with their intelligence. It seems as though, the killers were leading them on. By appearing in one place, which was to get Alan & Christian to follow them to a certain spot. Where another would appear going in the opposite direction. Which would cause the two of them to lose site of the first person they were following. Creating all sorts of confusion for them both. As the killers made a mockery of them by using this tactic as a way to torment them. Alan & Christian had no idea which of the three personators to pursuit.*

The goal was to break them apart, so that the killers could have the advantage. By getting each of them to follow two of the three personators dress in the Faces of Death attire. To seek out the results on whether they made the right choice. According to who is personating the killers & who isn't? If that's really the case according to Alan who is a master mind when it comes to this sort of thing. For all he knows! This little game with the Faces of Death masks could well be a distraction from seeing the real big picture. That his intuition serves him well by figuring out somewhat of the killers plans. However, it would be fair to warn Alan about the stipulations that can effect even the brilliant minds in which he processes. That the killer can manipulate the intelligence of one's mindset to something so far out of reach. That it effects a person's decision on whether they come to terms with understanding the killers motives. As Christian knew all so well of the conflict that can surfaces without warning. As Christian explain the situation to Alan that just when you think you know the stipulations to the game. It suddenly back fires in your face. Do to the fact that he experience it? Back at the galleria hall, one year ago on this exact same night. It was just as simple to not get ahead of themselves. That they must not feed into temptation or it may come back to haunt them.

Christian advise that they stay alert to their surrounding & to take one step at a time. That they should stick with the plan of finding the others before it is too late. The problem was? Is that they didn't know where to start looking. That's when Alan came up with the idea that he can locate each of the remaining cameras from a tracker build into his cellphone. Which would lead them straight to Lisa & the gang. In hopes of getting to them first before the killer does? They begin tracking the devices deep in the woods where they were hardly no one around. Which seems a bit strange to Alan who was pretty sure that the cameras weren't where they suppose to be. Alan is positive that someone move the cameras from it's original spot & place them in certain area's around the woods. Which seems kind of odd, considering the fact that it was Lisa's job to remove them. It suddenly dawn on them that maybe they were walking right into a trap. Which led them to believe that Lisa, Jason & Jerry made the same mistake. Figuring that the killers got a hold to them as well, which leaves the two of them. As they suddenly realize that the others didn't stand a chance. Do to the fact that they all didn't see it coming. Just as they begin to understand the logic of the games truth meaning of "I Spy"? They realize than the consequences that follows the game stipulations.

Once they realize that? Things begun to surface such as footsteps circling all around them. As they started to hear voices of their names being call from a distance. Also the fact that there were hidden cameras all around them. Capturing every aspect of it on camera. Leaving the two of them to wonder what will happen next? As their greatest fear was about to commence right before their very eyes. The two of them became highly alert to the commotion circling all around them. As they begin to see shadow figures moving amongst the trees. At that point, they both made the decision that now is a good time to run. In which, Christian succeeded in doing, while Alan had gotten the surprise of his life. When someone grab a hold of him to keep him from escaping. Christian then started to hear Alan calling out to him, but by then it was to late. As Christian bail on him. That he was too scare to even look back to see what is happening. Christian had no idea where he was running too, which puts him in more danger. In which he found himself in unfamiliar territory. It seems that the further he went into the woods, the more things got intense. Do to the fact that he was being hunted by prying eyes who has fixated their attention toward him. The fact that he was surrounded by shadow figures who seems to be ducking in & out of site.

Which cause a bit of confusion on Christian's behalf of not knowing what direction the assault would occur? The fact that it was too dark to see anything lurking around in the distances. That he would have to rely on instinct to get him out of this situation. The fact that he was under so much pressure? He couldn't even think straight on what to do at this point. Do to the issue that he was distracted by all of the commoition in the area. Christian didn't know what to expect to happen from all of this chaos. As he was experiencing some difficulties concerning to his greatest fear being recognize beyond belief. It was at that very moment where Christian would get the shock of his life. When the killer grab a hold of him from the blindsided. Which comes as no surprise? Do to all of the distractions that has capture his attention. That left Christian vulnerable to withstand the sudden attack by the killer. Who is determine to keep the momentum by sneaking up behind him, unexpectedly. Which led to a scuffle between the two of them. Come to find out that it was Jason behind the hideous mask. In fact, it was the exact same mask they use to scare Jason the other day? It was just a cover up to keep the killers off their trail. As Jill & the others came into the picture with masks on. Including Alan who seems to be okay.

Christian was relieve once he realize that the shadow figures were his friends & not a foe. As he come to realize that this was their only option. To fend off any potential threats that maybe lurking around. Jason simply explain to Christian that the masks camouflage them. That the killers aren't the only one's that can blend in with the crowd. As Jill handed Christian a mask to put on. So that the killers would have a difficult time trying to locate him amongst the crowd. Also to stay conceal from the cameras long enough, until they are able to remove every last one of them. By use the trackers on Alan & Jerry's cellphones to locate each one? It seems as if Lisa had a better solution about gettting rid of the cameras. That the only way is to shut them down one by one from the news van. It seems as if their little strategy work by disguising themselves to take part in the mayhem. By pretending to be an outsider, in order for them to get to the news van. Once they reach their destination? They didn't waste anytime disconnecting the device. Once they establish what was needed to cover their tracks? They then started to search the surveillance monitor to try & find some kind of evidence that would help answer one of the many questions. That would shed some light on this case. Lisa had look at every angle of the videos with the help of the others & came up with nothing. That is until? Something caught Jill's eyes on one of the monitors that would level the playing field?

CHAPTER 21

Discovering The Mystery

Which comes as a huge surprise that left Jill speechless on what she just discover. Not only did she spotted someone in the Faces of Death attire. She also discover the mystery behind the mask. Which comes as a bit of a shocker when she recognize the person behind mask number one. That left Jill mystify on the subject that there's a possibility the killer could be George Larusso? A long time film director at her school who is obsess with her. According to Jill's recollection? Jill simply gave a quick version that would explain her history with George. Stating that he is the one who led her on, the entire time by trying to get close to her. Which would explain this whole incident that connects him to the murders. That only a sick individual would do? In order to get rating for establishing what seems to be great entertainment at their expense. Which explains the situation with the cameras. Follow by the deaths of her friends Deshawn & Amanda who die in vain all because of her. That the monitor show a clear picture of him in the Faces of Death costume. It then became clear to them that the cameras play a huge part in discovering Lisa's secret. In which the killers were refering too, when they mention something concerning such a thing. Which was one way of letting them know that they are being study carefully by the use of Lisa's cameras.

Which was confiscated to help the killers keep taps on each one of them. Which makes all the sense in the world. Do to Larusso's history of experience behind the camera's. The thing they really wanted to know was what were his intentions. Which was one of the many question that needs to be answer? Which question their inner thought on the possibility that there's a purpose behind these killing. Which reminded Alan that he needed to tell Lisa about the concerns he has about Jill & the others. Figuring that one of them is responsible for the tragedies that is taking place. Which led the two of them to believe that Jill was the one the killers are after. Which was brought to her attention by Lisa who wanted an explanation. Which would explain Jill's connection to this George Larusso character. That there is more to the story than something simply as a crush. Jill on the other hand didn't have any explanation for Larusso's actions. That her guess was as good as theirs. Lisa & her crew decided to play devil's advocate to try & make sense of why this is happening. As they broke down every little detail that may shed some light in regards to how to approach this situation. Out of curiosity? Alan & Christian wanted to know how did Jill end up with Lisa, Jason & Jerry? When her job was to stay at the cabin, until they return.

Jill would then explain herself on why she left the cabin? Stating that she receive a text message from Deshawn's cellphone. Which was to inform her that the killers has set a trap & that her friends are walking right into it. Not knowing that it was the killer who sent her that text message? Which is the perfect solution as a way to conclude her in the mix. By creating the ultimate deception to lure her out into the opening. Where Jill would later discover that she was a pawn in the killers game. When she stumble across a video that was sent to her from Deshawn's cellphone. Showing video clips of Deshawn's dead body lying somewhere's in the bushes. Eventually, she got the message. The video also show clips of her being follow by this certain individual. Who is consider as a ghost at this point by using the crowd as their cover. Jill at that point felt threaten by the thought of being notice under the watchful eyes of the killer. Who is nearby keeping taps on her, which plays in the hands of the killers. The fact that the killers had the element of surprise on their side. Paranoia play a huge role of succumbing to the fear of facing the moment of truth. Unaware of the danger she now faces of being tormented by the killers who is lurking within the large crowd of people in attendance. Jill nearly had a close call when she spotted that certain someone in the scary goblin costume staring at her.

At that point? Jill begin to back away slowly, keeping a close eye on who she believe's is the killer. Jill however, found it to be very unusual that the killer didn't make no attempt to come after her. Which seems kind of strange that whoever it was behind the mask just stood there watching her. Which to her seems kind of creepy? Then again? This person in the goblin costume has been acting strange the entire night. However, just as Jill begin to get sidetrack by *the possibilities? The unexpected happens! When she was abducted by person's unknown by placing a sack over her head from behind. Jill would soon realize that this was for her own good. Unable to reveal themselves too her? Jill's kidnappers decided to let her in on the secret by whispering to her. Who they are? Which was her friends Lisa, Jason & Jerry who has disguise themselves in order to stay hidden from the killers. While they search for the cameras. Which was Jill's explanation for leaving the cabin. Which would answer Christian's & Alan's question on how she ended up with the others. Lisa came up with the idea to wear costumes in order to set the bar that they too can blend in with the crowd by disguising themselves. Until they are able to accomplish what they were set out to do? Which is to retrieve the remaining cameras that the killers confiscated.*

Which made Lisa realize their mistake? When the killers use Jill as bait to flush out her, Jason & Jerry. While it was made to believe that the killers would be in one of the faces of death costumes. If not in all three of them, in which the killers wanted them to believe such a thing. When all the while the killer had been in the same goblin costume the entire time. According to Jill's statement? Which allow the killers to spy on them all? Even with the masks on their faces. That they had been fool this entire time by thinking that they are two steps ahead of the killers. Which had them all second guessing certain things like for instant? Is Jill's friend Larusso is the real killer. That the actual killer had them all right where he or she wants them. That they must decide whether or not Larusso is the perpetrator. Who has led them all on a wild goose chase. Just as Jill describe earlier, containing to her encounter with him. As she too begin to question her remorse toward him. At that defining moment? They all realize that they weren't as close of solving the mystery. That the killers led them to believe that they were getting closer to the truth. When in fact they didn't have a clue on how far off they were. Their only option is to follow up on their leads. Which is to track all of Larusso's movement throughout the crowd. Which means that they would have to turn the cameras back on.

Which was their only option if they want to get to the bottom of this conspiracy. As they begin discussing among themselves the possibility that this game "I Spy"? Is nothing more than a gimmick to cause conflict. By making things appear to be something they are not? By all means? Keeping them from seeing the big picture. Which seems to be the conflict concerning the three masks. That connects together as a equal of one being. Which states the concept that the Faces of Death masks can do wonders. By conbining together as a force to be reckon with. Meaning that Lisa & the others are left to face the wrath of the three masks. As they try to uncover the truth? That they all must succumb to the fear that torment's them. Of the pain that will be issue out? In reference to the Faces of Death masks. That states each of the three masks description. Which has conbine together as the source. Which spells out trouble for the group, as they realize what they are up against. Lisa had then made a suggestion that maybe the cameras can be some use to them after all. Lisa explain? The plans to the others? In hopes of killing two birds with one stone? By capturing the three people in the Faces of Death costumes. By exposing them for who they really are? Depite the fact that one of them has already been reveal as one of Jill's friend. Which is George Larusso? The search now is for the two remaining masks that will uncover the mystery on who are the one's behind the wooden figures.

In order for this plan to work? Is if everyone do their part by participating. The object is to split up into two pairs of groups to stand a better chance. By having Alan & Jerry to keep an eye on the surveillance monitors. While keeping the others posted on what is going on around them. By communicating the information from the news van on to them. By using a special transmitter device that is use for special occasion such as this one. The object is to locate the three Faces of Death masks & to reveal the person underneath the costume. It is Alan & Jerry's job to lead them in the right direction. While the four of them search the crowd for the killers. It was Jill & Jason together as a pair & on the otherside it was Lisa & Christian who team up. Everyone seems prepare to do their part by collaborating together to uncover the truth. However, things didn't pan out as they planned. Do to the high percentage of people wearing scary costumes. That made it hard for Alan & Jerry to pinpoint the killers location. The downside of it all? Is that they didn't know whether the killers had change into another costume. Which can turn disastrous within the matter of seconds. Do to the fact that the killers could be standing right next to them. And they won't even know it? As Lisa & the others search the crowd for that certain someone who is probably stalking them in the process.

Which was one of the concerns that they now face by going the extra mile to seek the truth. Yet they realize the danger that comes with the territory. By playing in the hands of the killers who's expectation seems pretty far out. In reference to how it's all going to play out? The scary thing about this whole *ordeal is the psychological effect. That weights heavily on their brains of the thought that everyone is a suspect. That there's a good chance someone in the crowd. Who is circling around them. Isn't who they appear to be & could well be an imposter. Which is one of the contents of the game's true potential. Which is the downside of finding out the truth behind this conspiracy. That these are the steps they must follow in order to begin understanding the process? By sorting out the guilty ones that has disguise themselves. Jill decided that now is the time for George to come clean. That she was determine to get some sort of answer. Which would explain the reasons behind his behavior toward her. Which involves her two friends in the process. Which also places Jason in the mix. Do to the fact that he still had feeling for her & wanted to know what this guy problem was? They also wanted to know what was his connection in reference to the last two massacre that occur in their city & how it pertains to them. Which is the question that concerns them the most of what will be reveal.*

Confusion plays a huge role in all of this controversy that resulted to more conflict. That has inflicted a tremendous amount of anxiety that has weight heavily on their brains. Which was the one thing Jill couldn't understand, as she try to make sense of it all. On whether she was being misguided from the fact that what she saw is real. Based on what she witness when discovering the truth about her mentor George Larusso? Which was the thing that drove her insane momentarily. Until, she got sidetrack by her cellphone that had started to ring. Which is to inform her that she has a message. A message showing video clips of the news van, which is where Alan & Jerry are? Immediately they assume the worse, as Jason also receive the same message on his phone. They both try calling in to reach Alan or Jerry through the transmitter, but somehow the signal seem to fade. Leaving them to be expose to the harsh crowd where the killers rome. Jill wanted to go back to the news van to check on Alan & Jerry, but Jason insisted that they stay put. Until, farther notices? As Jason made the case that he didn't know when the killers posted the video & the time in which it was sent to them. For all he knows! They could be running right into a trap by going back to the van. In which the killers hopes they would do? Not knowing the stipulations that may occur?

CHAPTER 22

Worse Case Scenario

Of establishing some sort of scheme which would lure them right into the killers hands. By getting them to believe that the killers has set their sights on Alan & Jerry. Thinking that maybe Jill & Jason would come to their aid. Not for one second? Thinking about the possibility that they maybe already dead & the fact that the video. Is just a decoy to get Jill & Jason to take the bait. In hopes that it will entice them to see what is going on? Which is the killers plan? According to Jason's theory. As it turns out that his assumptions seems a bit off. As they both receive different clips showing two separate videos. Jill's cellphone show a video of someone in one of the three Faces of Death attire. Stabbing a certain individual who's identity wasn't reveal. That led the two of them to assume that the victim in the video was either Alan or Jerry. They also discover that it was the same mask that George had on. "Which is the mask of Pain"? Meanwhile, on Jason's cellphone show a entire different video. Which is a video showcasing them at the opportune moment in real time. Showing clips of them being shown that they are being follow by the killer. Who is recording their every move. The two of them begin to feel that discomfort feeling, as if though they were surrounded by all sort of prying eyes. As the mindgames suddenly became an issue.

Creating all sorts of mayhem for the two of them, as they try to make out who amongst the crowd is the killer. Which seems difficult to do when the crowd is emulating what the killers are doing. Which is taking a page out of the horror films by recreating the scenes from some of the most ruthless slashers names of all time. The main issue is that they didn't know what to look for? On whether they were expecting to see the Faces of Death masks or something out of the ordinary. As their minds begin to play tricks on them. Especially, when things is starting to take a turn for the worse. Like for example? Trying to getting in touch with Alan & Jerry for the first time since the signal faded. Which led them to believe that there was a reason they lost contact with Alan & Jerry. That the video they receive showing the news van explains it all? Which had them truly convince that it was the killers they were talking too & not Alan & Jerry. As they both fully knew what the killers are capable of? That it would be wise not to underestimate the killers capability to manipulate the situation. Jill thought that it would be a good idea to warn Christian & Lisa about what has transpired so far. So that they wouldn't fall for the trap that has been set. Jason just hopes that he can reach them in time.

It seems as if Jason got a hold to them just in the nick of time. However, just as Jason begin to explain the concept in which it contains to them? Jill had notice the creepy person in the goblin costume that stood a couple of feet away from them. Who appear to have something sharp in his or her hand at the time. At that moment, Jill try desperately to get Jason's attention, but he was to busy talking to Lisa & Christian on the phone to notices anything. Jill made a last attempt by yelling out Jason's name? In which he responded to the cry's of Jill's voice. As she made a break for it, with the killer hot on her trail. In which Jason made a late attempt to go after them. Do to the fact that he was caught off guard by it all. That eventually, he lost site of them in the chase. Which wasn't going to stop him in the least. Do to his persistent to find her no matter what the consequences maybe. On the other hand Jill found herself scambling through the crowd to get away from the killer. While at the same time yelling for someone in the crowd to help her. With the killer steady on her trail that motivated the crowd even more. Not knowing the seriousness of the situation. To them it seems like fun & games that they all enjoy. Which made her situation that much worse do to the fact that everyone she crosses wanted a piece of the action.

Putting Jill's life in jeopardy when everyone in the crowd surrounding her became a factor. By duplicating what's is expected of them. Which is to take part in the chase? In which she manage to avoid the killer in the process. Who has lost site of her in the mayhem. As so she thought? That she is not out of the woods yet! Taking that she is being chase by others, who could easily be the killer. DIsguise as one of the locals to throw her off. Which is the killers strategy for raising the sake. By baffling Jill with all sort of distractions that would effect her thinking. In result to the conflict that is weighing heavily on her brain. That all boils down to who she believe's is the killer. At that moment? Jill became distracted by her surrounding. Given the fact that she has attracted unwanted attention to herself in the process. Jill also notices all three members of the Faces of Death clan in the area. Who is circling all around her as she try to make her way out of the crowd. Which seems bad for Jill who found herself at a crossroads. Only to discover the seriousness of her situation based on how she look at things. Creating a major problem for her to withstand the pressure she is under. Of deciding her fate in which it all refers to how well Jill operates under these conditions. Refering to the phone call she receive from the killer the moment things took a turn for the worse.

At that point? The killer begin to inflict a tremendous amount of anxiety to scare Jill into believing the hype. With all of the mindgames that is being played on her. On who is the killer? Especially when she is being chase by person's unknown, which put a spin on things. Not to mention the three individuals in the Faces of Death attire who is constantly appearing in the crowd around her. Who also pose as a threat, which was mention by the killer. To give Jill that uneasy feeling that she is being hunted. However, before hanging up? The killer reminded Jill of the game "I Spy"? Which is to benefit the killer, as Jill must decide which individual in the Faces of Death attire is the perpetrator, if any for that matter. For all she knows the killer could be one of the people in the crowd who is chasing her. By pretending to be something they are not? Which effects her better judgement on what to expect to happened now that the stage has been set. That the killer couldn't plan a better setup than this. In order to keep Jill in the dark about what would happen next? Which is to witness first hand of the terror she must have felt. When the people around her begin taunting her by threating her with knifes. Once the word got out that there is a film being made starring her as the victim. By using the cameras from the news van to capture every shot. Also using the crowd as part of the show, which would define every aspect of the movie.

As it was made clear to her that the person behind the scenes is George Larusso. Instantly, things started to make sense to Jill, as she put things in perspective? The only thing she couldn't make out. Is what was his involvement that places him in the midst of things? On the other hand? Jill didn't have the time to focus her attention on the matter. Do to the fact that she was caught in the middle of a crisis. It was made clear that the videos of them were being uploaded to everyone's phone. Clearly they all seem in denial of realizing the truth about what's been taking place as of late. That they couldn't take a hint of what is being display right before their very eyes. By disguising the big picture, which blindside the crowd from seeing the truth. In which the killer seems so good at doing? Meanwhile, Jill found herself stranded with no place to go? Things begun to look grim for Jill, as she was stop dead in her tracks by the sudden movement of a swinging blade. That nearly was inches away from her face. Do to the fact that she wasn't paying attention. At that point? Jill became disorient that she had no idea where she was going. That landed her in a predicament she wasn't prepare for. With a shocking twist that would change the concept of the term "Fear"! Which was at that defining moment where words alone doesn't describe how sadistic this game can turn out to be.

Having to deal with all sorts of confrontation within the crowd of people. Who seem aggressive toward her, which plays in the hands of the killer. Who has use this opportunity to seize the moment. By affecting Jill's mind with all sorts of irrational thoughts on what should she be looking out for. Considering her circumstance of being hunted by the unknown. Which led to the final detail that would put a spin on things. When Jill receive a text message on her phone. Stating that her worse fear is about to commence. Leaving her with these final words? Which is what is her favorite scary moment in a movie where something horrific happens? Within that second of reading the end of the message. Jill receive an unexpected encounter with fear, as she got the surprise of a lifetime. When someone intervene by grabbing a hold of Jill to avoid her from being stab by the killer. Who bearly miss her by a inch, thanks to the good samaritan. Jill, at that point became a loose cannon, despite the fact that she had no idea what was happening. Until it was too late? The person that came to her aid was Christian & Lisa? Who reach her in time in order to spoil the killer's plans. Thanks to Alan & Jerry quick thinking. By informing the others about Jill's situation, which stated the fact that it was Alan & Jerry speaking with them & not the killers. As the killer once again turns the tables by flipping the script.

By having Jill to believe that it was the killers who confiscated the news van. Thanks to the video she receive from them, showing someone being stab to death. Who she thought was Alan or Jerry? Which has led up to this point, where Jill & Christian found themselves on the verge of death. As the killer came charging toward them both. Once Jill & Christian slip & fell to the ground. The moment Christian pull Jill away from harm, which gave the killer the advantage over the two of them. Which leaves them little time to react to the assault being made. Including Lisa for that matter who try to get the two of them back on their feet. Just as things begun to look grim for the three of them. In comes help from Jason who appear on the scene to lend a hand. By engaging in a nasty scuffle with the killer over total supremacy. Jason would soon receive some assistance from Lisa. Which gave him the upper hand in the fight. That eventually led to the down fall of the killer, as Jason took full advantage of the situation. By stabbing the killer multiple of times in the chest. As the blood begin to flow rapidly from the lacerations that is being inflicted on this person. An enraged Jason" became out of control by his fury of hatred toward this person. With the crowd in his ear cheering him on. Which didn't make things any easier for him. It all came down to the voice of reason from his friends to get him to lighten up a bit.

Once they got Jason to calm down a bit. The thought had enter their mind on who is behind the mask. Everyone at that point became silent as the moment of truth was about to be reveal. Behind the mask was a guy who they didn't recognize to be the killer. Do to the fact that they didn't have no idea who this person was? Figuring that maybe the killer has pull the wool over their eyes once again. By using certain people in the crowd as a pawn in his or her twisted game. As a decoy to setup a opening to advance to the next stage of the game. By putting innocent lives at stake. The fact that all eyes is on Jason, considering the fact that he had murder someone. As the crowd was in disbelief about what they just witness. As Jason was left with the guilt of murdering a innocent man. Who just stood there over the decease body with the victim's blood on his hands. Blinded by rage! Jason took it upon himself to get even with the killer. Not knowing the repercussions that may occur? Which is the statement the killer was trying to make by painting a picture that would express the true concept of the game. As Jason & the others receive a text message from the killer stating the words "Gotcha". As the person who was stab begin to come too, making light of the situation by coughing up fake blood. As it turns out that this whole thing was nothing but a scam.

CHAPTER 23

The Enemy Within

By poking fun of the situation that makes for great entertainment at their expense. By turning the tables on them, as a way to express the true nature in which it is portray. Refering to the videos of them being film by the so called killer who is capturing some of the most defining moments in filmmaking history. According to the crowd who seem amuse by it all & wanted to take part in the event. As a way to exploit Jason & the others weaknesses. Which is the process the killers is aiming for? Which shows a different side of them when face with emotions. That demonstrates the conduct in which it is perceive by the different mood swings they must have encounter. When the pressure was on? At the heat of the moment where instincts takes over. Creating the enemy within, which was display by Jason. As he wasn't at all impress with the guy who pose as the killer. In fact, Jason was so upset that he express how he really feels. By wanting to kill this guy for real. As a way to relate the message to the crowd that this is not a game. It took Jill to get him to calm down a bit. At that point? Lisa saw no point in continuing their search for the killer. Do to the fact that it would seem impossible to get everyone to cooperate with them. Which gave Lisa the idea that if they can't get to the killers. Than she would get the killers to come to them.

By getting all three of the individuals dress in the Faces of Death costume. To emerge in front of the cameras so that Alan & Jerry could keep taps on the three of them. In which they were successful in doing by flipping the script on the killers. By following in their footsteps that relates to the quote "The hunters has how become the hunted"? As Jill & the others were now on the hunt to unmasked the potential killers. As they all speculate who the two possible suspects are? That had them leaning toward George as one of the suspects in this case. While there was no doubt that the person in the scary goblin costume was consider, as a possibility? Do to certain issue that this person could well be the killer. Which seems sort of tricky because there is no speculations that the two of them are the actual killers. Therefore, they would have to look outside the box? Do to the other two Faces of Death masks they didn't account for? Or the crowd for that matter! Do to the fact that they had no idea what to look for? Considering the people who is behind it all, that makes it that much difficult to resolve the issue. That results to conspiracy, as credit to the game "I Spy"? Which sents out all sorts of confusion that penetrates a person's way of thinking. Between the four of them? Their only option was to go after the remaining two suspects who's identity remains anonymous? As the four of them split up in groups of two's in order to reveal the mystery behind the Faces of Death masks?

With the help of Alan & Jerry who has located the killers position. As they past on the information to Jill & Jason who was trailing one of the suspects. While Christian & Lisa was on the hunt for the other one. Between both groups, they stood a good distance from the killers. In order to maintain the course of action by pursuing in the killers footsteps to see where would it lead them. For their sake? The possibility of revealing the secret to who it is behind the mask. At times! they manage to lose site of the killer momentarily. Do to the large crowd in attendances that sidetrack them with all of the pranks being play. Still! the killer had no idea he or she was being follow. At least to their knowledge? Meanwhile, back at the news van, Alan & Jerry notices that the cameras begin to shut down one by one. Until, they lost coverage of the live feed. Which they depended on to help solve this thing. Eventually, the cameras begin to showcase the live feed again. However, doing the time when the cameras was off. Things begin to get serious as emotions ran wild. As of what was their next move if they had no eyes to rely on to get them through this? Which was the issue concerning their friends lives, that was at sake. Within those three minutes the cameras was off? Played a huge momentum swing on things. That had them all expecting the worse on how certain things would turn out.

The only explanation Alan & Jerry could come up with, when the others ask him? What went wrong! Is that there was a malfunction with the cameras of some kind of glitch in the system. Which is a very normal thing that can occur occasionally with this sort of equipment. Which didn't seem as no big deal at the time. As they continue on with the search to reveal the two people behind the Faces of Death masks. Somehow, they manage to lose site of the killers trail. Once the cameras went off? Which places their four friends in danger of being expose out in the opening. With no sign of the killers in site that may cause for some concern on their part. Do to the issue that the killers may have change their appearance once again? Under the circumstances that they knew what was happening the whole time. Which gave them the chance to slip into something new, while the cameras was off. Putting them in great position to counter attack Jill & the others who is unaware of the danger that lurks within the crowd. Which is the perfect setting for the killers. Who has the element of surprise on their side. Of not knowing what to expect, when there is danger taking form all around them. That is shaping up to be one huge problem for Jill & the others. Do to the fact that the killers has drop off the radar & that they are at the mercy of the crowd.

Which is one way for the killers to camouflage themselves by adapting to the environment. Which is suitable for the killers who took full advantage of the opportunities that was presented to them. Which was one way of looking at it? As Jill & Jason, along with Christian & Lisa took to the bad news. As a sure way of being out number by a large margin of people. Who is enlighten by the killers actions! Which encourage them to do the same. Which doesn't make things any easier for the four of them. As they must take certain steps in order to come away from this thing unharm. However, as the four of them begin to carefully make their way through the crowd to get back to the news van. Chaos ensues? As the crowd begin to form a circle nearby. A couple of feet away from them. That had them "asking questions" about what is going on? In which, Alan & Jerry didn't have no recollection of? Do to the fact that it hasn't show up on the cameras. Which seems kind of odd of how they could miss this sort of thing. Being that it didn't pop up on the monitors. That had the two of them wondering just what Lisa & the others is yapping about. Concerning to something that they don't see on the monitor. Which is crazy? Considering the fact that they are not seeing, what the four of them are seeing.

Only to discover that the cameras are not picking up the area where all the focus seems to be. Do to the fact that it was happening away from the cameras. Which seems like the only explanation at this point. Which didn't seem all that amusing to them, considering how it all seem too familiar. Of someone playing a cruel joke, in order to seek attention. Once the joke was over? Everyone resume where they left off? As if nothing had happened. Not long before than? Alan & Jerry spotted the killers again on the monitor. As the two of them past along the message to Jill & the others. To maintain their search to uncover the truth. Which created a problem between them all, as there were some miscalculations on the behalf of both sides. Mainly because of the misunderstanding that has them all seeing things that isn't there? Like how Alan is trying to guide Jill & Jason toward the killer. To an area where the killer seems non existence. Which also seems to be the case with Jerry? Who is helping Christian & Lisa, locate a killer who isn't where he or she suppose to be? Taking to consideration that the cameras doesn't lie. The fact that they are in plain view of the killers position. According to Alan & Jerry's standards? That it would seem impossible for them not to see the two masks that contains to the Faces of Death attire.

Something is obviously wrong with this picture, as of how the four of them couldn't detect the killers movement. Within the area where they were spotted at? By Alan & Jerry who seem pretty sure of themselves, do to the evidence that is being shown from the monitors. Which shows evidence of them in pursuit of the two killers. Which didn't seems to be the case with the four of them who had no visual of the killers. Which had them all detecting that something seems to be out of place. Alan & Jerry got straight to work on the surveillance video, in order to resolve the issue. To their surprise! Was the defining moment of the night. Where the killers had somehow override the system by replaying the video from before the cameras went off. Giving the killers more than enough time to premeditate their next move. Which was the reason why the cameras shut down. Cutting the live feed, which is the reason why they had trouble figuring out the video. When there was live action within the crowd. Causing them to miss what took place within the circle a few minutes ago? They manage to fix the problem, but the damage had already been done. Of not knowing the extend of what is at stake now that they are in the dark. Of what's to come? They couldn't make heads or tails on what to expect, now that the stage has been set.

Considering the circumstances of how it would effect the outcome. In which it define's the true meaning of how the three masks operates. In reference to how manipulative the killers can be? Creating all sorts of diversions in order to conceal further observation. By doing whatever's necessary to keep things confine within the rules of the game. Considering that there are no limitations to how the game is perceive. Which is the concept that all things are excepted, no matter the conditions. Considering the manner in which it was presented. Creating turmoil, in which Alan & Jerry wasn't perpare for? To make matters worse? The killer decided to send a message to them both? Stating that there has been some changes to the game. As the killers made some stipulations that would decide their friends fate. Depending on their skills, considering that this is what they do best. Which gave the killers the idea to play a game called " Hide & Seek". The rules were simple. Considering the fact that Alan & Jerry must seek out the killers, as they hide amongst the crowd. "The catch" Is that they must figure out certain details? Given to them that would lead them to the killers. With the help of their friends? Who is still making their way through the crowd.

The goal is to steer the two groups on the hunt to seek out the killers. Based on the clues given by the killers that would get them closer to the truth. Which seems impossible! Do to the amount of distractions surrounding them. Making things all so difficult to stay focus on the task at hand. The thing is that they had no knowledge of the killers current output. Considering that they had two options to choose from. Based on the clues that is given. Which can turn out as the right choice, depending on what clue they decide to go with. Which can also be a bad choice if choosing the wrong path. That it was Alan & Jerry's job to help their team make it out alive. Considering that their friends life is in jeopardy. Based on Alan & Jerry's skills of surviving the fittest. As the killers wanted to know, which team would benefit from this opportunity. If any for that matter? On one hand? There is the team of Alan, which includes Jill & Jason. While on the otherside lies Jerry's team. Which is none other than Christian & Lisa. Who saw no purpose in taking part in this event. However, if they didn't participate in this event, then there would be consequences for their actions. Which left them no other alternative. Figuring that something good can come from this? Beside the fact that there's a possibility this whole thing could be a setup to lure them into a trap.

CHAPTER 24

Unknown Enemies

Which was one of the many concerns they are face with that creates tension for them all. Do to the amount of pressure they are under. That they must live up to the game's expectations in order to receive any kind of indication that would shed some light on this case. It was just the question of? Who would benefit from this once in a life time opportunity. Between the two teams? It was as simple of who wants it more? Considering what they are willing to do. In order to seek out the truth behind the mystery itself. The game of "Hide & Seek" is the perfect format to provide them with such information. Based on the clues that may have some implication to how it all would play out in the end. A game with all sorts of stipulations that can affect the outcome. In result to the missing link that remains hidden away amongst the crowd. Making the situation that much harder to deal with. The fact that they couldn't function well with all of the distractions in the area. As they begin bearing down on the potential suspects. According to the clues they choose to follow. That had them going around in circles. The fact that they couldn't decide on who to pursue. As the killers perform a bit of strategy to make things a little interesting. By including all three of the Faces of Death masks into the picture. Along with the slicker costume from the movie "I know what you did last summer". Not to mention the costume from the movie "Urban Legends".

In which the killers were seeing in both attires? That made the situation that much difficult to bare. Which turn out to be sort of a guessing game to try & confuse them. Which is the concept of the game's true interpretation. By reflecting the realization that certain rules doesn't applied? When things begin to get shaky? When the environment itself begin to change along with everything else. Considering the fact that the crowd has made themselves known. By participating in the killers gameplan. Which is a major problem! Now that the killers has provided the crowd with the privilege to participate in the game as well. If that wasn't terrifying enough? Then just think about the mindset they endure. When they heard a storm developing in the distance. Words alone doesn't describe how ironic things became within a few seconds. The fact that they couldn't make heads or tails on who is the killer. Despite the fact that they couldn't identify the one's responsible. All because they didn't know who to look for. Considering the issue with the previous masks that the killers has worn. Yet alone? The other scary masks that is being displayed in the crowd that they must account for? Which creates one huge disturbance for Jill & the others. As they try to remain calm enlight of the situation. Which is the conflict that resemble the Faces of Death masks.

Containing to how the three masks operate, in regards to it's definition concerning to the many ways it can effect the mind. That may cause a person to be delusional, which is the purpose behind this game. Stating the fact that the killers had this entire thing plan out right from the beginning. Planning out every detail down to the wire. By arranging every aspect, in order for the environment to adapt within the killers design. Which is discomforting for both teams, as they realize what is at sake. The fact that they are now? The center of attention, which was Jill's main concern. The fact that she knew the whole time. What the consequences would be if they attended this party. That now is not the time to say "I told you so" when in fact the object is to not get sidetrack. Which can be severe if they lose focus of what's important. That being on the look out for any signs that would lead them to the killers. Who I might add? Is making it difficult for both teams. By having Alan & Jerry do the impossible. When there are lives at sake, who is depending on the two of them to succeed. Where others have fail? By pointing out the obvious, that it is pointless to obtain something that is so far out of their reach. To the point where Alan & Jerry started to question their abilities.

Of how it was made clear to them that they were no match for the killers. Being that they couldn't begin to understand the logic behind these games. That the killers are so good at disguising the issue. To where everything begin to take form on how things are starting to unfold right before their eyes. The fact that they are in way over their heads. As the two of them saw that it was pointless to continue the search. All because things begin to get out of hand within the *crowd. Come to find out that this whole charade was all for nothing? The fact that the killers has misled them all by having them doing the impossible of trying to seek out certain individuals. Who's object was to distract them long enough to obtain the element of surprise? Which invaded their minds with absolute fear, once Alan & Jerry figure out what was going on. All the while, they were entertain by the killers bogus scam. In order to keep them in the dark about what's to come? That had them all succumb to the fear, which haunts them. The fact that they couldn't shake that eerie feeling of being tormented by the killers. Things seem fine & dandy knowing that Alan & Jerry has the four of them in plain site. However, the fact of the matter is who was watching Alan & Jerry. As they help warn Lisa & the others about what to expect from the crowd.*

It was obviously clear that the two of them were so wrap up in the moment of protecting the others. That they didn't think about their own safety? Which was brought to their attention when one of the camera's that was fixated on the van. Had suddenly went blank? Causing a malfunction within the surveilance video system. That effected all of the cameras in the process. In result to them all on the verge of shutting down, once again. Figuring that it is the killers who has hack into their system from an unknown source. That is feeding off their data base, which is how the killers stumble upon their little secret. Which was the opening Alan & Jerry needed to track down the hacker. By using their computer skills to seek out the signal in the device use by the killers to confiscate information from the news van. It seems as if the signal was come from an area near the van. Alan & Jerry just knew that the killer would slip up? It was just a matter of time before their plan would work. It was just as simple as to lock in on the device. Once the killers hack into the system again & trace it back to the source itself. Which brought them to the killers location. It was just the matter of who will go & who will stay? Just in case the cameras come back on. The decision was left up to a game of" Rock, Paper, Scissors.

In which Jerry won by the way & decided to make a surprise visit to uncover the truth behind the one's responible. Which was the moment they have been waiting for? That finally? Their hard work is about to pay off do to their persistent. As Alan related the message to the two groups. About what just transpire, even though, the cameras were off. That disable him from seeing what is going on, which is the downside of it all. Of not being able to anticipate the killers movement. Which is precisely what the killer wanted them to do, as Alan realize their mistake? The moment he was contacted by the killer who decided to give him a call. Concerning the issue? In which the killer seen very optimistic about the outcome of this game of" Hide & Seek. Which now involves them all? It was just a matter of who is the one being hunted. The fact that the killers is hiding amongst them. Only to seek them out, one by one? Which is the object of the game's true concept. That it is up to him to save his friends lives, yet alone, himself for that matter. Which pertains to the many forms of the different stages in references to fear itself? Yet alone? The mind games that plays a huge part in it all. That has Alan on the verge of fatigue. As the killer begin tormenting him over the phone by describing in plain details that someone's life hangs in the balance. That it is up to him to determine which of his friends is being targeted. As the killer gave him an ultimatum by senting him video clips of each one of his friends being pursue? Including Jerry for that matter? That he must decide which video is accurate?

Which was the turning point for Alan, as he decided to pay less attention to the killer. Who begins laughing! The moment Alan hung up the phone. However, before ending the call, the killer advise that he make good on the choices he makes, considering who the killer is after? Refering too the footage showcasing his friends being under the watchful eyes of the killers. Immediately! Alan try to warn Jerry on the walkie talkie about the danger headed his way. Jerry however, found that the device they were tracking was one of their own. The fact that they were tracking something that belongs to them. In which the killers has confiscated from their van to use as leverage. In order to create a diverison that would define all odds. Especially, when the odds are stack against you? Of trying to decide which video footage is the most accurate that contains to the stalker who is in full pursuit of his friends. Alan also warn the others about the danger they now face. Considering the fact that they are in the middle of the chaos. That there was nothing more he can do for them, now that the cameras are no use to him. The fact that he can't update them about what is going on around them. Which left Jill & the others in the dark about the many concerns they may have on certain issue, such as this? You couldn't imagine the discomfort they must have endure in all of this madness.

Considering the predicament they are in? Which define's all odds on where they stand at this point. The fact that this whole thing was premeditated by the killers. Who's purpose was to deceive them by flipping the script. In order to make things a little interesting on how it would all play out in the end.

According to how well Alan & Jerry respond to the challenge of resolving the issue. Which could decide the fate on how the outcome is to be determine. Therefore, the outcome of this game is now on Alan's shoulders to step up. It was sort of like a game of "Chess"? Where the killers would make a move & it was up to Alan to counter that move with one of his own. It wasn't long before than when Alan heard someone knocking on the side of the news van. Instantly! He assume that it was Jerry outside of the van. Who seem to have made it back from investigating the area. To his surprise! There was no sign of Jerry anywhere's to be found. Alan would take it upon himself to step out of the van to see who it was knocking. He would then begin to call out into the dark for Jerry. As it turns out that he wasn't getting no responds in return. The only responds Alan heard was the violent storm that begun to form in the area. However, just as Alan turn around to get back into the van. He spotted a note that was left on the door of the van. With his name written on the front of it.

At that point? Alan begin to look around the area, as he took down the note. Feeling as though, he was being watch from a distance. Once he retrieve the note that was left for him to read. He quickly step back inside of the van & close the door behind him. Alan didn't waste anytime with opening up the note to see what it says? Alan seems confuse by it all? Taking that he didn't know what to make of it. As the note read "Life is a chain & that every chain has a link"? So the goal is to connect the links to the chain of events? It also read at the bottom of the note "Checkmate"? Not long before than? The cameras begin to come back on, one by one. It seems as though, they were back in business. Even though, he seem puzzle by it all? Of what the killers is planning next. Alan try to contact Jerry multiple of times before realizing the device that they were tracking looks as if it's on the move. That had Alan anticipating that it was Jerry who was carrying around the device. Even though, it seems as if Alan couldn't pick him up on the monitors. Which was okay! Because he had Jerry on the radar. Tracking him as he move along the area. However, Alan manage to track down Lisa & the others on the monitors. As he fill them in on the note he receive from the killer explaining the whole "life is a chain" deal. In hopes that Lisa & the others could help him figure out what it means.

CHAPTER 25

Panic Attack

The only explanation that seems rational that would explain the context in which the note was written. Which is the basic form of how this whole thing connects together. By linking together the murders that folllows the path in how it all relates to the chain of events. That would give them a better understanding about what is going on? The fact that this is right up Lisa & her teams alley. To solve the mystery behind the writing on the wall that confines them. On getting to the bottom of this conspiracy, in order to obtain some kind of linkage. That defines all odds on making a discovery that would shed some light on this case. Considering if they are up for the challenge that was provided too them by the killer. After all? This is what they do best? No matter how difficult things may seem. It was made clear to them that now is not the time to try & take on the matter. When the first thing they should do is to regroup & strategize from there. The first order of business is to locate Jerry, which wasn't no big deal. As Alan had him on the radar, tracking his every move. Thanks to the device he had confiscated in the woods near the news van. It was just the matter of guiding Lisa & the others to his location. Which seems a bit shady for Alan who is having a rough time fixating the proper spot. Where the device seems to be poping up all over the place. Almost as if the device is being exchange from one place to another.

That has them all confuse on the matter? Sending them on a wild goose chase. By misleading them from one area to the next. As the radar show the sudden changes being made by the device that ended up shifting unpredicably throughout the crowd. Making things all so complicated to resolve the issue, containing to their friend's survival. As they all had that mix emotions of

114

uncertainty? Thinking to themselves that this is just another one of the killers games. To throw them off track by creating a diversion. In order to keep things a bit intriguing on their behalf? That has Alan & the others dumbfounded by the cleverness of the killers strategy. Which wasn't nothing! Compare to what is about to happened next? Which would create turmoil amongst the environment. As Alan witness first hand the downfall of his friend's demise. As he saw Jerry stumbling into the crowd. Yelling to everyone that the killer is after him. Who looks as if he had been through hell & back by the trauma he suffer? Enlight of the killer's fury? That tells the story. Which didn't have any effect on the crowd, who consider it as some sort of prank being played. Even though, it has that realization feeling to it? Which makes it that much amusing to some of them. As someone in the crowd? Yell out the words that would send everyone into a frenzy.

That turn disastrous for Jerry, as he was bum rush by a hand full of people. Who felt the need to create a scene by going along with the flow. Taken that this is some sort of game that seems all to familiar to them. That led to the stabbing! Which created all sorts of turmoil for Alan as he try to figure this thing out. As a swarm of people block out the image of Jerry on the monitors. Making it difficult for Alan to see what is happening to his buddy. Lisa & the others try getting to him as well, but unfortunately, that didn't happpen. Do to the amount of people that made it tough on them to get through to him. As they too wanted to know what is with all of the commotion. Jerry on the other hand? Found himself on the receiving end of a bad predicament. That somewhere's in the middle of the mayhem lies the killers. Who excel at this sort of thing by adapting within the habitat, which makes them seem invisible. According to how well they can blend in with the scenery that favors them in every way. Which is the opening the killers needed in order to downplay the amount of people participating in the stabbing. That plays a huge role on how to disguise certain features that would benefit the killers. Which didn't look good for Jerry who is being mauled by the crowd. Which eventually led to his downfall of being stab to death by the killers. Who took full advantage of the opportunity without being discover. By using the crowd as their shield.

It was all fun & games until, that critical moment when they all realize that something wasn't right. When the crowd discover that there was no sign of life coming from the victim. The reaction from the crowd seem very high-strung, as panic spread throughout the area. Causing all sorts of turmoil within the crowd, as they did what was rational? Which is to get the hell out of dodge? While anticipating the fact that the killers are lurking amongst them. Which spreads fear throughout the crowd. Do to the speculations that the killers are somewhere's in the shadows of the madness. Making it hard for Alan to identify a potential suspect. As all hell broke loose? That creates a problem for him, as he trys to locate a needle in a haystack. While at the same time keeping a close eye on his friends. Who he seem to have lost in the chaos by the many of people that have ruin any chance they had of finding the killers. All seem lost at this point, of trying to establish some kind of common ground. That would explain how the killers are always two steps ahead of them. It seems as if the killers are putting them in a position. In order to carry out the next step in their plans & that they are stupid enough to fall right into it. Almost as if this entire thing was premeditate, as they follow in the killers footsteps. Of all the games being played in the process that led up to this moment.

Seeing that there was no point in continuing using the surveillance video. Alan decided to take his chances on going out to look for the others. He had no time to disconnect the equipment, so he left everything the way it was? Pressure was beginning to build? As the search became intense to the point where Alan had to weather the storm. Whether it was from being pananoid by hallucination or the fact that it was from the storm itself. That has affected his way of thinking, which is the mindset he had to endure. It's crazy how things change when you put a dead body in the middle of the crowd. Of all the different response given to such emotions that can trigger a panic attack. That had Alan concern about his own safety? Being that he would have to be extremely careful not to let down his guard. Considering that he is surrounded by pandemonium & that the killers are so good at disguising themselves to this sort of thing. He would soon receive a call from the killer. Who advise him to reconsider the continuation on revealing the truth behind the mystery. Based on how things would surfaces? Considering how the truth may play out? According to how he approach certain steps that can send him into a tailspin. Only to find the truth to be a blur. That may cost Alan his life in the process? Which was one of the many concerns in the discussion.

Of all the mindgames being inserted into his mind, which is the concept the killer is aiming for? As the killer reminded him of the fear that consumes him. Which is the mindset of how lethal the killers can be? Leaving him to wonder what is his greatest fear of all, before ending the call? A sudden chill came over him, as a strong gust of wind begin to take to the air by the upcoming storm that has taken form. As the fog begin to set in, making the situation that much difficult for Alan to visualize what's in front of him. Which makes the conditions that much scarier! As Alan knew all so well about the stipulations that follows. Knowing that he is in deeply over his head by the sudden discomfort he endure. However, it seems as if Alan came up with a solution that would reunite him with the others. As the thought enter his mind about the scanner that is place inside of Lisa's cellphone. Which the three of them share, in order to keep track of one another. Just in case they lose track of one another. Which is a brilliant move on their part, even though, Jerry is no longer with them. Which leaves the two of them to clean up this mess. Alan didn't waste anytime with going after the others. As he race to the area where they were. Which seems to be inside of a cornfield, according to the signal. Where majority of the crowd seems to be running toward to escape the killers fury.

Alan seem skeptical about entering the confines of the cornfield. Based on the fact that he may lose his sense of direction. While, going out on the limb in search for the others. Which didn't leave him no other alternative. Considering the fact that maybe the killer is already on the prowl? It seems as if the deeper he went into the cornfield, the thicker the fog got? Which disable him completely from seeing what's ahead. Leaving him at a disadvantaged of trying to anticipate the killers moves. Considering all of the commotion that is surrounding him. Which is the thing that concerns him the most. Do to the fact that he couldn't see what was going on around him. That had him second guessing his decision about entering the cornfield. Which was a little too late to turn back now! As he must continue on with the search of locating the others. Alan had no idea where he was going? As he begin to close in on Lisa's & the others position. Once he got close enough to the area where Lisa was? He begin calling out to her, hoping that he would get a response. However, that didn't happened? Do to the noise in the background that over exceeded his voice. However, he did receive some feedback. Which wasn't the response he was looking for? As he started to hear voices of his name being call in the distance. Which was spoken in a soft tone of voice that only he can hear.

It seems as if the voices was coming from all over the area where he was standing. As he starts to experience a great deal of fear. Considering how it effects his mindset of embracing the difficulty that has transpired. That left *him pondering on whether this was a figment of his imagination. That led Alan to believe that he was drawn in by the killers. Who may have confiscated Lisa's cellphone & if that's the case. Then it would mean the end for Alan, as he was warn not to proceed any further? Which cause him to panic! Do to the amount of pressure he was under. Being that he couldn't see who it was calling his name? As he was stun by the thought of having someone grab a hold of him. That send him into a frantic state of mind. Which was too close for comforter? As he come to realize that it was Lisa, who grab a hold to him. You couldn't imagine the load that was lifted from his chest. As he was relieve to see that it was Lisa & company. Who manage to stick together throughout the mayhem. As they manage to united as one, once again. Considering that now is the time to put their heads together, in order to solve this thing. Once & for all? Which brought up the situation involving Jerry's killer. As Lisa wanted to know did Alan catch the one's responsible for the murder of their fellow comrade. Alan response was sort of limited. As he explain that there were so many participant. That he couldn't tell which of them was the actual killer.*

Considering all that went on? Which is part of the design created by the killers. Who establish some sort of arrangement, so that everything can fall into place. Almost as if they are being tested? Which is the motive behind these killing, based on the perception of each victim. As the killers carefully observe each of them, in order to fulfill their quota. By including them as part of the scheme, in order to obtain the advantage. By using the victims background, as a stepping stone to set them up. Which is the reason why each of their friends death had been in vain. As Lisa & Alan both came up with the concept that they all are being study quite closely by the killers. Who knows their flaws! Which is the downside of it all, considering the danger they now face. That adds even more conflict within the case. In which they weren't able to discuss at the moment. Do to the fact that the storm had begun to get worse by the minute. That it was only a matter of time before it starts to pour down raining. Which is the least of their problems? Based on the killers footsteps that is lurking within the shadows of the cornfield. As they all could feel that unpleasant vide of the killers presence in the area. According to the movements in the cornfield that surrounds them. That has them all edgy about not having the ability to see what is developing around them. Which is sort of scary in a way, considering the mindgames of being unable to predict the resulting conclusion in this closing moment.

CHAPTER 26

The Haunted Cornfield

Which is the deciding factor on how this would determine each of their fate. According to the choices they make that can decide the outcome of the game. By testing their abilities, in order to reveal the secrets behind the mystery? Considering the fact that there will be consequences taken in the process. The further they search for the truth? That may have some repercussions, as a result to their actions? Leaving them with a unpleasant vibe, as they try to make their way through the cornfield. Feeling as though? The cornfield is haunted by it's eerie output. That makes a statement! Based on the conditions that has an affect on this entire situation. That has Jill, Jason & Christian concern about the many possibilities of something horrific happening. Considering that they are no strangers to this sort of thing. That there's some sort of catch to the mystery. Which will end with a question mark? Making it impossible! To collect any evidence on the suspects. Who is steady leaving behind trails of blood in the midst of these killings. Which seems to be connected somehow? Considering the fact that every life has a link in the chain. Which is chain together as a whole that compares a bondage between each of them? Which is the very thing they need to reslove if they want to seek the truth. About what is really going on? Which links them all to this so called chain that the killers speaks of?

As they seem puzzle by it all? Do to the fact that they let it sink in for a moment. Only to realize the truth of the matter, which is that they are confine within the cornfield massive estate. Surrounded by the heavy fog with a storm taking form overhead. Which speaks for itself? As they all begin to experience the torment of the killers wrath. As the killers made their presence known from certain stand points. Creating a tremendous amount of fear in the atmosphere of the many danger's they now face. The fact that they are not alone in the cornfield. As they were join by others from the party who seek to take cover in the cornfield as well. Which has dominated their sense of ability. Do to the many circumstances they had to endure. By being victimize constantly from other people who just appear out of nowhere's within the heavy fog. Which is unexpected! According to the sudden fears of what's to become of them. As the mindgames played a huge role in all of this chaos. Do to all of the distractions in the area that has set them apart from realization. It was at that moment! Where dominance would effect the minds of Jill & the others. When they begin to hear whispers in the wind. Follow by the movements in the cornfield, which surrounds them. Making matters worse than they already are? That defines a person's greatest fear in the most relentless way.

That came crashing down when Jill felt something unusual behind her. The moment she begin to back away slowly to escape the voices in the distance. As she could hear the ruckus behind her. Assuming that there is someone standing behind her. Almost as if she could feel the presence of that certain individual near her. That send them all into a frenzy, when Jill started to scream. Do to the fact that they were unaware of the circumstances at the time. Only to discover that it was just a scarecrow Jill encounter. Which is kind of understandable of how Jill could of mistakenly pass it off as a real person. According to the features that make it all seem real. They all were relieve that it was just a false alarm. Even though, they weren't out of the woods yet? So Lisa & the others begin to strategize what needs to be done. In order to make it out alive? However, the discussion was put on hold. Once Christian discover that the scarecrow was missing? As they all try to determine what had happen to the scarecrow. Which leaves only one explanation? That being the case of mistaken identity. As they all were deceive by the appearance of something so obvious. That it stand out in every way? In order to remain conceal within the confines of the cornfield. The fact that the killers are using any means to stay hidden in the shadows.

By adapting to the new setting, which is suitable for the killers to blend right in? Just as a lizard would when it changes it's colors. In order to blend in with the background, as a way to hunt & keep predators away. Considering that the same could be said, about the killers. Who's only objective is to hunt down their victims by changing their appearance, constantly. While at the same time keep a low profile from prying eyes. Who wants to expose them in *the process. Which seems impossible! According to the disadvantage Jill & the others sustain that requires certain aspects. That would led them to some sort of facts that would break open this story. In the meanwhile, the pressure was beginning to build. As they took on more than they could handle. Which is the question in itself of how far are they willing to go? In order to piece together the missing segments to the puzzle. That would explain the contents, in which it is perceive. The fact that the "Faces of Death" masks is link to this entire investigation. Which is the solution to the murders that defines the mystery behind the truth of the matter. That the answer lies waiting nearby in the cornfield. Where there were sighting of other scarecrows in the area as well. Which is mind-boggling! Considering the difficulties they had to endure. Of trying to sort out this debacle of a mess. Only this time? They decided to stick together for a change. After all, they knew that this wasn't going to be a walk in the park, sort of deal?*

That there will be moments where the unexpected may occur in the process. Considering all of the commotion that is taking place around them. Which is the thing that concerns them the most. Of being unable to predict the outcome of what's to come. Having to deal with the blindness of the fog. None the less? The storm that is developing overhead. That would send chills down a person's body for sure. Considering all that can go wrong? Meanwhile, as they try to search for a way out of the cornfield. A sudden feeling came over them. Feeling as though, they are being watch by each one of the scarecrow they come across. As they couldn't help, but to feel, as if the eyes of the scarecrow were following them in the process. It seems as if the further they went into the cornfield the more bizarre things got. As they begin to speculate that something doesn't seem right? Especially! When the unexpected occurs. When Jill notices that one of the scarecrow's seems a bit different from before. Almost as if the creepy figure move on it's own. That led everyone to pause for a second? While they investigate the ins & out of the scarecrow. Which does more than to scare off birds. As Jason would soon find out the truth about the mystery containing to the scarecrow. When he got up close to the creature's face. Only to witness the type of fear that would dominate a person's state of mind.

That all came crashing down right before their very eyes. That cause a rift within the group. As things begin to fall apart? Basically, when they all got sidetrack by the scarecrow, which was the opening the killers needed. In order to carry out their plans. Which is the element of surprise? When literally! The scarecrow reach out unexpectedly at Jason. Who was caught off guard by the sudden attack. As the others were surprise by the scarecrow responds. Which created turmoil between them within that split second. As Alan was snatch violently into the thick fog from behind by another killer. Which was around the same time Jason became a victim himself. Which led to a split second decision on what's the best knowledgeable thing to do at this point. Which divided the group as Lisa went after Alan. While Jill & Christian stood behind to free Jason from the killer's deadly grip. Somehow, they manage to get him down from the wooden stand that the scarecrow was hook on. The three of them didn't waste anytime with going after Lisa. Who was out searching for Alan within the confines of the cornfield. At some point doing the search the three manage to lose site of one another. Which became a problem for each of them. Do to the agreement that they made to each other about staying together, no matter the consequences. Which now! Is endangering the mission. Considering that now they are not accountable for one another.

Which leaves a bit of uncertainty? In every aspect concerning the outcome to this conclusion. That decide's the fate of each one of them. Depending on the path they choose to follow that can end in one or two ways? In Lisa's case she chose to go after Alan, despite the fact that they were suppose to stick together. Which now puts them all at risk? By separating herself from the group. Knowing! This is what the killers wanted? In order to maintain the thrill of the game. Which can be unpredictable at times. Which now puts her at the mercy of the cornfield. As Lisa use her cellphone to track down Alan where'a'bouts from a tracking device that was inserted into his phone. Not for one second? Thinking of the consequences that may occur? That can lead to a downward spiral, if not careful. Which brings up Jill, Jason & Christian for that matter, who follow in Lisa's footsteps. Which didn't end good for the three of them. As they found themselves stranded in the fog. With the mindset that they must choose a path to follow. Now that the stage has been set to coordinate the finishing touches to the segment of the game. That each of them are hold accountable for the path of their choosing. Which isn't at all going to be easy, considering the difficulties they are left to face. Which is where the Faces of Death masks come into play. The fact that they will be tested by each of the masks description of "Fear, Pain & torment".

Which is the three symptoms that indicate's a certain discomforter that has to deal with emotions. Especially! The affect it has on the brain of not being able *to function properly when under duress. Which is all part of the game & it's entirety. It was just the matter of how they would measure up to the standards. According to the path they choose to follow? Which is the deciding factor of where it may lead them too. The fact that fear, pain & torment plays a huge role in all of this controversy. Which brings up Lisa's situation? The fact that she is blinded by her own ambition. To the point where she seems desperate. In hopes that she can find her companion. By tracking his cellphone? Which could be in the possession of the killer. Who is probably leading her on? Which could very well cause her downfall. While, the same could be said, about Jason. Who assume that it was Jill & Christian behind him. As he made his way through the cornfield, in search for Lisa & Alan. Until, that moment? Where Jason discover that something wasn't right. From the moment he turn around to see that there was no one in site. That whoever was behind him stop the same time, he did? Which had him wondering that if it wasn't Jill & Christian behind him. Then who was it? That has been trailing him this whole time. That's when the mindgames begin to take affect. The fact that there were some movements in the area around him.*

Which arouse his curiosity even more through the sense that perhaps he is being pursuit. In the attempt to catch him when he least expected. Which seems like the typical thing to do? However, it seems as if things didn't turn out that way. As Jason started to hear Jill's voice in the distance. At this point? Jason seem skeptical about the whole thing. Figuring that maybe it's a trap to lure him right into a bad situation. Which is a decision he had to make himself? On whether he should go down that road. The fact that he knew first hand what the killers are capable of? Considering the many ways they could manipulate you. As the thought enter his mind that maybe he is playing right into the killer's hands. Which doesn't concerns him at this point? That all he could think of was Jill. That it is his job to protect her, no matter what the case maybe. At that point? He made the decision to go after her. Meanwhile, Christian seem a bit tense about things. Only because it reminded him of the night he spent in the Galleria Hall. The fact that he was blinded by the illusions that had him thinking deja'vu all over again. Feeling as though, he was back at the room of smoking mirrors. With all of the heavy fog that surrounds him. In the middle of the cornfield, with all of the chaos confine within that area. Having the thought of not knowing what to expect. When the inevitable is a sure thing. Which is one of the scariest moments, in history when the unthinkable happens.

CHAPTER 27

The Sum of All Fears

Which defines the sum of all fears when there is so much that could go wrong. Which pretty sums up the solution to Christian's problem. The fact that he is being taunted by fear within the surrounding area. From various individuals who wouldn't stop at nothing. Until, it was declare that fear is recommended, as a result to the conflict within him. The fact that he could hear the whispering in the wind, but was unable to rely on his sense of ability to see what has taken form around him. Which is literally blinding him from seeing the truth in all of this commotion. The fact that Christian would have to take extreme measures. In order to remain cautious of the killers who has set their sights on him. As things begun to take a turn for the worse. When reality sets in, that there is no avoiding the killers wrath. However, in this case? There seems to be a slight of confusion with this whole ordeal. When Christian found himself in a bit of a predicament. The moment he receive a phone call from Alan's cellphone. In which, Lisa is currently tracking at the moment. Which seems to be in the possession of the killer. Which means that Lisa is falling right into the killers hands. By allegedly being drawn in, under false pretense. Which weighed heavily on Christian's mind. As he could hear the killer laughing wickedly in the background. Without wasting anymore time? None the less. Christian did what was expected of him. Which is to try & warn Lisa about the danger that is headed her way.

Christian try repeatedly to get in touch with her through the phone, but fail to do so? Considering that there is a busy signal each time he calls. To make matters worse! Christian's battery begins to die out on his cellphone. As he made a final attempt to reach her before it is too late. Somehow, he luck up

& manage to send out a text message. To warn her of the danger she now face. Which is no guarantee that she would get the message in time. With his phone out & all? He had no way of knowing if she was okay. Christian's only option now! Is to make it out of the cornfield unscathed. Meanwhile, Lisa found herself wandering in the shadows of the cornfield. Hoping to catch up with her long time colleague. Not realizing that she is tracking the killer in the process. Who by the way is making things difficult for her to pinpoint the actual location of Alan's cellphone. Do to the fact that it is poping up all over the surrounding area. From one place to the other? Until, it eventually came to a halt? Which was around the same time she receive Christian's text message. Once she got the info about what is going on. Lisa then realize, her mistake? The fact that she has been tagging along behind the killer this whole time. Which maybe the last mistake she will ever make? Which led to the chase, as she realize that the indicator on Alan's phone. Begin moving toward her location at a rapid paced. As the roles were reverse & that the killer was now tracking her. At that point? Lisa took off running in the cornfield, with no knowledge of where she is running too. Which is the thing that scares her the most.

Considering the possibility that something unexpectedly could happened in the process. However, the thing that would create a even more dramatic spin on things. Is losing the signal to Alan's cellphone. Which puts her in a tough position. Do to the fact that she has lost base with the killer. Who could be anywhere's at this point? Knowing that she is being watch, takes a toll on her psychologically. Which affect the mindset in ways that would have a person seem delusional based on the mindgames that is being played on her. When the reality is? That Lisa has succumb to her worse fear of all. Which is being tormented by fear itself of all the things that could go wrong. When the setting itself seems a bit creepy. Do to all of the distractions in the area she have to deal with. Being confine within the cornfield is one thing, but having to deal with the blindness of the fog & the bad weather. Doesn't make things any easier on her? Somehow, she manage her way through the cornfield & found herself back at the news van. Where she discover that someone had been snooping around inside of the van. By the look of things? Lisa swore that it was Alan who was in the van. As it turns out? That she was right on the money. When she notices a note that was from Alan. Which would explain everything that has transpire so far. Which is storage on a flash drive near the computer, that read "play me"?

Once she uploaded the information onto the computer. Things begin to unravel as she discover some footage containing to last years massacre. Which involves around Thomas & Jasmine's disappearance. The fact that the two of them were setup by person's unknown. Do to some footage that was shown of them at the Galleria Hall. That started, when all hell broke loose between the four of them of trying to sort out the confusion. When they all was dress in the same costume. Nearly seconds away from killing one another. That resulted in a conflict when one of the masks accidentally gets yank off? Revealing the people behind the Ghost Face masks. As you well know! Were Jasmine follow by Christian, Jill & Thomas. As they all started to reveal themselves one by one. However, somewhere doing the discussion between Jill, Christian, Eric & Jason? About the secrets behind the Faces of Death masks. Jasmine & Thomas seem to have slip through one of the two way mirrors, unnoticed. Which was refer as "The Mirrors Of Verification"? Which happened just before the altercation between Jason & the killer. Who wore the same costume as Jason. Which was from the movie"Friday the thirteen? Who seem determine to make things difficult for them in the end? By creating turmoil to insinuate the outcome. By capturing Jasmine & Thomas attention when they saw a note with their names on it? That was on the mirror that had rotated. Where they were standing up at? Which was to lure the two of them in position. In order to trigger the mechanism. That would rotate the mirror once again sending them on the inside of the mirror. The instant they took down the note. It happened so quick, within a blink of an eye? That Jill & the others seem puzzle by it all? As of how the two of them manage to disappear without a trace. With the four of them standing there with their backs turn to them. Which seems very unusual?

However, the situation became critical, once they discover the note that the killer had left for them to read. Which was on the otherside of the mirror. The moment the mirror rotated? Sending Jasmine & Thomas on the inside of the mirror. That created turmoil within the group. As time was of the essence to find the two of them. Before the time expires of determining Thomas & Jasmine's fate. Which eventually led up to the spectuation that Jasmine & Thomas were the one's behind the murders. When there were no traces of their where'a'bouts? Which was the killer's trump card to throw everyone else off? Do to the circumstances of how it all was perceived? Considering how it all when down. Which had to deal with a lot of controversy once the discovery was made.That Jasmine & Thomas were the master minds behind it all? Considering how it was believed that it was Thomas who attack Jason. A short *while after their disappearance? Which led up to the final act? When Jill step in to resolve the issue by firing shots at both Jason & the killer with a gun she found. All because she was put in a difficult situation. That she had no control over? Do to the circumstances at that time. Which resulted in more conflict when discovering at least thirty other bodies with the same costume on, as Jason & the killer. However, just before the incident occur with Jason. Lisa witness the unseen footage of Jasmine & Thomas being murder within the confines of the secret compartment of the mirror. By the same individual who attack Jason minutes later. Which was the opening the killer needed, in order to set the stage to draw open the curtains. Behind the scenes that would explain the conspiracy concerning the disappearance of Jasmine & Thomas. Which arouse everyone's suspicions that the two of them just maybe the prime suspects in this case. Leaving Jasmine & Thomas to take the fall? While the real killers escape the scene of crime. At that point? Lisa finally got the scoop she needed to address the media. The only problem is that she didn't have a face to go along with the murders. As that part still remains a mystery?*

However, just as she was getting ready to leave the news van. To reveal the breaking news to the others about what she just witness. Her phone begins to ring? It seems as if the call was coming from Alan's cellphone. Lisa seem skeptical at first about answering the call. Knowing! who it is? That is on the receiving end of the call. Lisa then" Decided to answer the phone. Only because she had a few questions of her own that needed to be answer, but at what price? Which is the question in itself? Of what the consequences maybe in result to her seeking out the truth. As the killer gave her an ultimatum to choose from? The fact that she is willing to go deeper in the mind of the killer. In order to get what she wants? Which is at the expense of her friends. Who is made to suffer the consequences, do to her persistence. Although, it may seems as if Lisa is sacrificing her friends in the process. Do to some questions that needs to be answer, which may not be accurate. Seeming that the killer is full of mindgames. Which fell on dead ears for Lisa who is no amateur to this sort of thing. As she too had a card up her sleeve. By keeping taps on each of them, thanks to the quick thinking of Alan & Jerry. By suggesting that she keep taps on Jason & Christian. By switching their cellphones with identical replacements that have a tracking device planted inside of it. While the installment was already place inside of Jill's cellphone the one Lisa sent to her as a gift. By claiming to be her secret admirer?

Which allows her to track each of them down from any & all devices she has in her possession. As Lisa made another discovery about how the killers were able to downplay the whole secret admirer deal. By monitoring the people around Jill, Jason & Christian. In order to see where each of them stand. Which is how the killers knew about Lisa & her crew. That all the while Lisa & her crew were studying Jill & her friends. The killers was studying them? Which kind of backfire in their faces, as the joke was on them. Which is how the killer was able to take full advantage of the situation. With the thing that Lisa generated with talks of a secret admirer. That the killer pickup on & has use it to his or her advantage? Which says a lot about the people she is trying to seek out? Meanwhile, the tracker on Lisa's cellphone begin to pickup Alan's signal again. Only this time? It seems as if the tracker from Alan's cellphone. Seems to be headed in a different direction from her. As the killer left Lisa with an ultimatum on which of her three friends is the target. That the answer she seeks depends on the outcome of her choice. As the killer pinpoint each of their location. Which indicated that all three of them is being track down. By three different tracking devices that has each of them in site. Which is up to her to decide which one of the three trackers is the most accurate. Considering the fact that she has three choices to choose from. Which plays in the hands of the killer who left Lisa to decide which of her friends are in danger. It was at that defining moment? Where she begins to experience the side efffects of Fear, Torment & Pain all in one dose. Which effects the mind with absolute fear considering the circumstances. The fact that the killer has them all figure out. That there was nothing the killer didn't know about them.

As the killer made it plain & clear to her that the answers involving these murders. Lies within one of the three remaining survivors of last year's halloween massacre. Before ending the call? Clearly! It sums up the solution that there's a connection between the killer & one of the three people she has been investigating. Being that the three people the killer were refering too are none other than Jill, Jason & Christian. From that very moment, Lisa made it her duty to seek the truth no matter what? However, Lisa was still left with a decision? That it is up to her to choose which of them is the target. Which led her to consider each of them as a liability. Do to the circumstances? In Jill's case? She seems a bit over protective about her life. Not letting anyone inside? Which is a big deal considering how the killer is always after her. On the other hand? Jason seem a bit on the edgy side. Almost as if he is hiding *something. Considering how he is always in enrage with anger? Then there is Christian! Who has problems dealing with certain issues. Which kind of having him jumping into conclusion everytime something happens? Who seem sort of skeptical about things in general? Which explains a lot, considering what she has come up with so far about the three of them? Lisa didn't have anytime to figure out who's involve in all of this. When there are three lives at stake that needs her assistance. If she is willing to take the risk of doing whatever it takes. In search for the truth behind the mystery, which evolve's around the three of them. Clearly! She had no insight about what is going on. Considering the fact that she would soon find out. As the pressure was beginning to build substantially?*

At that point? Lisa made an attempt to go after the three of them. Surely! She knew that there was a good chance the killer is watching her in the process. Which is why she remain cautious by using the news van. As a way to ensure her well-being, while searching the cornfield for the others. Even though, she had a difficult time figuring out. Which of her three friends is she tracking. Perhaps, it could be the killer? That Lisa is tracking for all she knows. As she didn't put anything past the killer on what & what not to expect. When there is so much at stake? Which is why she went out of her way to take extreme precaution. By slowly driving through the cornfield, in hopes of not killing anyone. Do to the fact that there are innocent bystanders in the area as well. Throughout it all, Lisa manage to track down one of them. Which one! Is the question? At that moment? Lisa had stop the van to take a look around to see who she had track down. Lisa then, begin to call out in the distance. As she waited for a response, but unfortunately, that didn't happen. All she heard was silence, which is scary in itself. Do to the circumstances of thee unknown. Which is the barrier that stands in her way of proceeding any farther. That the promise that was made to her is about to reveal itself? Depending on the intake on her interpretation of the truth. Which is the measuring stick of how she uncovers the mystery. Depending on the way she looks at things from a different perspective.

CHAPTER 28

The Ending Results

Which is the defining moment of the concept in reference to the truth. Of what's is to become of Jill, Jason & Christian for that matter? Which by the way? Is totally up to her on how things would turn out for the three of them. The fact that each of their lives is in her hands. These were the sort of thoughts that ran through her mind. As she continue to call out in the distance to see who it is on the monitor. That she supposedly track down? Lisa then detected movement from the target, as the tracker on the monitor begins to move toward her location. However, somewhere's doing the search? Lisa manage to lose the signal in the process. The fact that she lost track of one of her friends position. Which seems kind of odd, do to the fact that one minute ago the signal was there. Then the next? It just disappear without a trace. Which seems to be all part of the killer's strategy. In order to confuse her psychologically about the deciding factor of the game. Being that she is determine to seek out the truth. Which can also determine her fate as well? Which depends on how far she willing to go & at what price? That would decide the outcome of the game, according to the path she choose. Which is the scariest part of it all? Do to the fact that she has no idea about how this story is going to end? As Lisa kind of understood where Christian was coming from? When he describe to her in plain details of the conflict he face back at the Galleria hall that night. When he was trying to understand the mystery containing to the truth of why this is happening.

Surely! Lisa knew that she is well qualify to handle a case such as this one. Do to her experience in this sort of field that she excels at quite often. However, she also knew when to pick her opportunities & this wasn't one of them. Lisa then, decided to head back to the news van. Do to the fact that she didn't know what to make of the situation. Involving the sudden lost of her friend signal. Which made her think twice about searching for something that isn't no long there. Feeling as though, the killer is leading her on? Which made her think twice about exceeding any further down an unknown path. That may have some repercussions, as the situation became intense. Things became complicated for Lisa. The moment she got back into the van & drove off. Only to discover that she is being track by the same signal she was tracking before. Who she assume was one of her friends. Only to find out later, that it was all part of a scam to lure her back into the mix. Being that the hunter is now the hunted. As the monitor on her phone show traces of the signal following her. Almost as if the signal has lock onto her position. Which makes it difficult for her to lose the pursuer. Who is steady on her trail by making every move she attempts. Which seems impossible? According to Lisa, who decided that enough was enough? As she went ahead & stop the van to see who it is? That is pursuing her? It was at that moment where she discover the truth about her belove assistance Alan. Who fell onto the hood of the van the moment she hit the brakes.

Suddenly, it became clear to Lisa that the person who was pursuing her this whole time. Was no one other than Alan, who's body has been place on top of the van. Do to the fact that he been murder in the process. Considering all of the blood that was smear on the window. Which all boils down to her feeling guilty about the death of her co-worker & friend. Feeling as though, it was her fault by getting in too deep. Which results to the demise of her two loyal companions. In which she feels totally responsible for? By having that sort of burden on her conscience. Which is the price she has to pay when there are consequences for her actions. Considering the cause & effect method? In which she come to realize the procedure of the game for which it stands. That she must succumb to the realization of determining the fate of her three friends. The fact that she dug her own grave with all of her self-made decisions. That landed her deeper within the confines of her own disarray. That her persistence! Has effected lives in the process. Which all came bearing down on her when a shadow figure appear behind her. Clearly, Lisa had no idea that she is being stalk in the process. It seems as if this person waited for the opportune moment to select the best time to strike. Where the opportunity would present itself. Which is suitable for the killer to saw his or her opportunity to seize the moment. At that point? Lisa found herself in a bit of a predicament. As she was caught off guard by the sudden appearance of the killer. Who appear as a scarecrow that had threaten her life by applying a sickle across her throat.

Who had suggested that she follow orders & maintain her composure. Clearly, she wasn't able to move, but manage to take a peek through the rear mirror at the suspect. Which is how she knew about the scarecrow costume. Lisa then, starts to speculate that Jill & her friends was a decoy? That it was the killer she was tracking all this time. As the killer had her believing that it was one of them she was tracking. Which gave the killer the opportunity to sneak inside of the van. The moment she went looking for one of them. It seems as if the signal she was picking up was actually the killer's. Who was leading her on all the while long. That before the killer snuck into the van. He or she place the tracker on Alan's body. Who was already dead as a doornail on top of the van. Which is why she lost the signal momentarily? Being that she couldn't understand why the signal seems to be following her every move? As the killer use Alan as a decoy? To keep Lisa attention on the monitor, so that the killer can sneak up on her unexpectedly? Which is the perfect setup? Considering the output in which it was portray. Considering that she didn't know what to make of the situation with the tracker following her every move. When the truth of the matter was that the killer devise a plan. To where he or she can confiscate her without any hassle. Everything that has happened so far, was all part of the killer's plan. The fact that she was lure under false pretense. Which enable her to follow in the killer's footsteps. By having Lisa to believe that her friends were in danger. Do to some persuasion from the signals on the monitors that indicated the facts. In which she proceed to follow causing all sorts of miscalculations on her part. Which led the killer right to her. Considering that this was all part of the plan from the get-go? The plan to draw her right into the confines of this barrier that prevents her from uncovering the truth.

That sort of backfire the moment she decided to take matters into her own hands. Which has endanger the lives around her. That has affected her way of thinking considering the chioces she has made so far. Which is why she is made to suffer the consequences. All because of her willingness of seeking the truth. When the truth of the matter is that she uncover the contexts for how the game is to be decided? The fact that the killers are playing according to each of their weaknesses. Which is how the killers has maintain the game so far. Which has landed her in the hands of the killer. Who plan out every aspect, in hopes that they would take the bait. Considering that the killers could go on forever. Based on their actions which perceive them. And on that note? Lisa had a chioce to make considering her predicament. It was the matter of kill or be killed that this point. As she begin to hear sirens in the distance. It was at that point where Lisa decided to take a stand against the killer. When she instantly slam on the brakes, causing the killer to lose his or her balance. Which was the break she needed to escape the killer's grasp. Even though, the stunt she pull left her with a scar when the killer grazes her neck with the sickle. Which could of ended badly if it wasn't for the seat belt. In which the sickle got tangled up in, the instant she hit the brakes. That led up to the chase where the killer was in hot pursuit of Lisa.

Until, that defining moment where karma plays a huge role that would decide the outcome in the chase. Where the advantage would be in Lisa's favor? When she came upon the police, who was inches away from shooting her. Do to the situation of being blinded by the fog within the cornfield. However, the same couldn't be said? About her pursuer who was reduce to a hail of gunfire. In regards to Lisa's plea to the police that the killer is after her. Which was the signal? The police needed to open fire on the potential suspect. What a sign of relief Lisa must have felt when the police ran a check around the surrounding area. To make sure that there was no other surprises. However, at this crucial moment, Lisa main focus now was to reveal the person behind the mask. Which seems to be the main focus on everyone's mind. To see who is the one responsible for all these murders. Which would shed some light on this case? In hopes that it will lead them to the other suspect in the gruesome murders. As it turns out? That the killer behind the scarecrow mask was no one other than Louis. Which was the person the police were looking for? Do to the fact that he turn up missing the night after his girlfriend Ashley was murder. Which was at last year's halloween massacre. Considering the fact that he wasn't seen or heard from since then. Until now? Which seems kind of odd considering how things are starting to unfold. However, the real question relies on his involvement in connection to the murders. Of what was his motive behind these killings.

Which led the police to search him to see if they could find anything that would help uncover the mystery. In doing so, they manage to find a cellphone along with a blank disc that had been use to copy something. As it turns out? That the cellphone belongs to Lisa's co-worker Alan. Who was mauled by the killer. Who they believe was Louis? As the police was still trying to sort out the evidences to confirm that it was him. The police would soon get the proof they

133

needed the moment they enter the disc into the computer. Which took place inside of the news van. That verify Louis as the killer. As the disc show footage of him taking off one of the three Faces of Death masks. Which was the Mask of Pain? The same mask George had on? Jill's secret admirer? Who she claims is out to get her. As Lisa come to realize who the second suspect is? To her surprise! Things didn't pan out the way she thought it would? Being that George Larusso was Eric's private investigator. Who was looking into his case & that Jill was part of his assignment. Considering the fact that Jason & Christian was part of Lisa & her crew assignment. As the police thought that it would be a good idea if they put two experts on the case. By having two different agents working the same case? Which comes as no surprise to Lisa who knows how this sort of task works. Being that she too shares the same interest. However, things still wasn't becoming clear to Lisa, as of why Louis & George had on the same costume. As that part didn't set straight with her. The police simply explain to her that in order to catch the killer.

George job was to pose as the killer by wearing the mask of pain. In order to get close enough to the killer, which ended badly for him. As the killer was two steps ahead of him. By planning out the scenario for him to take the fall. Framing George as the killer while the real killer gets away. Only to later find out that it was Louis who killed George which was all shown on the video. Which was the only explanation the police could give to Lisa concerning the case. Being that the two of them had on the same costume. According to the details provided by the video. Which explains the issue with the surveillance cameras. And how the killers try to put the blame on George. Speaking of which? Lisa had forgotten that she too have some footage of her own. That have to deal with last year's mix up. Concerning Jasmine & Thomas involvement in the killings. Which was a blessing from her dear friend Alan before he died. Which is to clear the air about Jasmine & Thomas involvement. Which was shown to the police on how Louis & his mystery partner set the two of them up to take the fall. Just like they try to do with George. Only this time! Lisa manage to catch on to what they were doing & decided to expose them. As she also come to realize that Louis was indeed Alan's killer. All do to some speculations that it was Louis who confiscated Alan in the cornfield earlier. Who brought him back to the news van, in hopes of retrieving any evidence that they may have of him. Which led Lisa to believe that this is why the equipment in news van seem so out of place. The moment she step foot out of the cornfield & back to where the news van was?

As she continue to prove her case to the police that Louis made it look as if Alan. Purposely left the flash drive device on the counter. In order for her to see what he wanted her to see. Which is to stir up more controversy on who is the killer? Considering that Jasmine & Thomas was a non factor in this case. That the two of them were just a pawn in the killers game. So was Jason & George for that matter? The purpose of the device was to frame George as the killer. Just as he did with Jasmine & Thomas. Which is why he had Alan's cellphone & the disc on him. Doing the time he was kill? That it was his duty to tie up all the loose ends. That pose as a threat to him. Which is why Louis was determine to get rid of her. Do to the fact that she was a threat to him. While his partner-in-crime attend to other concerns. Which seems to evolve around three special individuals. Who's lives hang in the balance? Following last year's massacre of unfinished business. Which notify the police to make preparations to rescue the three remaining targets. The call had came in? That they manage to get a hold to one of the victims. Who they confirm was Christian, but had trouble locating the other two victims. As Lisa release the names of the two victims to the police. In hopes that they could get to them in time. Which brings up Jill & Jason situation. The fact that Jill receive an unexpected call from the killer. Who is up to his or her normal routine as usual. Which is to inflict her brain with more chaos, none the less, with all sorts of mindgames.

CHAPTER 29

The Moral of the Story

That has affected her way of thinking considering the amount of pressure she is under. Do to the fact that the killer has that instinctive on how to be persuasive, if need be? In order to carry out his or her plans. Which is the method the killer use to manipulate her. By threating to kill her before the night is over. As the killer couldn't stress enough, in plain details of a game called "Hide & Seek. Where the killer would hide amongst the cornfield. While seeking out Jill's every move depending on her footsteps. It was then? Where the killer decided to take it a step further. By referring to her that she is being observe very closely. As the killer begin to share some information describing her appearance. Down to every detail? Which is mind-boggling considering the creepiness of having no visual awareness of the person who is watching you? Which was the signal for her to take off running. Even though, she could hear footsteps tagging along behind her. Which made it difficult for Jill to look back to see who it was behind her. As her main focus was to make clear of the killer who is in hot pursuit. Which seems to be the case, based on what has transpire. However, doing the chase Jill manage to lose her cellphone in the process. Somehow she manage to get a break. When she stumbles toward a opening within the cornfield. Which led Jill to a creepy abandon house. Where the property is surrounded by the cornfield. Even though, she could still hear the ruckus coming from within the cornfield. As Jill assume that her stalker is lurking around the surrounding area.

Waiting for the opportune moment to strike when she least expects it? It was around that same time when Jason receive a surprise of his own. When he came face to face with a scarecrow that had on a hockey mask. From "Friday the thirteen movie. The exact same mask he had worn prior to last year's halloween massacre. Follow by a note that is attach to the scarecrow. Which is to inform him about the truth behind these killings. The fact that someone is making a mockery of him. Based on the message the killer was trying to send? By posting up something that defines logic? Mainly, to prepare him for what's coming next? Which contains a video from the killer of Jill stranded nearby. The purpose of the video is to inform Jason that his ex-girlfriend is being prey upon. That in order to save her? He must participate in a game that involves around Jill's life span. A game of cat & mouse called "Catch me if you Can"? It was then, where the killer struck a chord with Jason. The instant he realize that Jill was in danger. He then took off to find her, but was obstructed by the police. Who intervene? Which ended in a conflict between the police & Jason. Who was tase by the police all because he fail to apply to the orders that was given to him. Who didn't give him a chance to explain what is going on? Which in his mind pretty sums up Jill's fate? That there was nothing more he can do to save her. Until, Lisa & Christian got involve. Who demanded that they take it easy with him.

Meanwhile, Jill found herself in the middle of a crisis, as things begun to get intense. Jill figure that the only way she can remain safe is to enter the abandon house. The house itself seems spooky enough. Which freak her out completely do to the fact that she is surrounded by darkness. That there were all sorts of weird noises coming from the house. Which is kind of understandable. Considering the fact that it's an old house that squeaks. However, there was that possibility that all is not what it attends to be? Which led Jill to believe that there is someone inside of the house along with her. As she just had that feeling that something isn't right. Which brought Jill's attention to the broken mirror beside her. Which in her mind? Seems like protection, as she stare down at the long sharp object. Thinking to herself that this could be the straw that breaks the camel's back. Now that she is prepare to defend herself from any sudden attacks. However, when Jill bent down to grab the broken glass? She suddenly found herself being grab from behind. By someone's who had a tight grip on her. At that point? Jill somehow manage to take a glimpse at her attacker from the corner of her eye. It seems as if her attacker is no one other than. The person who was dress in the scary goblin attire. Who seems to be pretty aggressive in the scuffle, in order to maintain control over her. It seems as if things didn't turn out the way the killer hope? Being the fighter that she is? Jill manage to break free from the killer's grip & just went berserk. Stabbing the killer multiple of times in the chest, until her attacker could no longer stand.

Which didn't slow her down a bit, even when the suspect appear to be dead. It was up to Jason to get her to calm down & to remove what was left of the glass from her hands. As he come to realize that she sustain some cuts to her hands in the process. Do to the amount of pressure she apply on the glass. That rip through her flesh as she was motioning the object back & forward. It seems as if the police miss the confrontation between the two parties involve in the scuffle by mere minutes. That by the time they arrive it was too late. Which is a total lost, considering the moral of this story. That will remain a mystery on why this even occur. However, there was some speculation about who is the one behind the goblin mask. Considering that this person has been acting strange all night long. That Lisa & the others finally get to see who it is behind the mask? As the police slowly approach the suspect with caution. They come to learn that this person had it in for Jill? As they discover a knife near the suspect along with Jill's cellphone that she lost in the cornfield. In which the police confiscated as evidence. In hopes that it will lead them to something useful. The time had finally came to reveal the person behind the killings. You couldn't imagine the look that shock them all? On who the second suspect is? Which was a bit of a surprise to them all? As Lisa pull back the mask & reveal that the killer was Eric Johnson. The man that pulled the wool over everyone's eyes with his innocents.

Which comes as no surprise to the police who suspected that it was him all along. It was just the matter of time before he slips up. Which put a spin on things considering all of the mix emotions about Eric's involvement in these killings. Jill & Christian seem lost for words. As of how this whole thing turn out. The fact that Jill found it to be outright disappointing that Eric would attack her. After the story he laid on them one year ago. Involving him being setup by the killer who turn out to be him all the while long. Jason on the other hand seem blindsided by it all? Considering all of the things they have been through. Which has now come down to this moment? Which is where Lisa comes in. To resolve the issue containing to the justification within reasoning. In order for the three of them to get a better understanding about things. Lisa had shown them the footage from one year ago in the Galleria Hall. That explains everything that when on that night. Involving the truth about Jasmine & Thomas run in with the killer. Who was recently identify as Louis. Which comes as another surprise to the three of them. *The fact that the two of them come off as a wolf dress in sheep's clothing. Which was the metaphor they use to formulate their plan. By disguising themselves in order to blend in with the environment. Which is the perfect formula to undergo on halloween. Which is why Lisa comes as a professional investigator. Do to her brilliant intelligence mind that can resolve any issue.*

However, there is still were some issues that remains? One being the motives behind these killings. The fact that there are links to the chain that still doesn't add up. Like the issue involving the death surrounding Eric's private investigator George Larusso. Which brought up another subject that contains to Jill? As Jill come to learn that she was part of an investigation by her alleged stalker. Who turn out to be a undercover agent that has been watching her from the start. Which is how Eric knew about everything that has been going on, so far. By using George as a resource, in order to retrieve personal information from him. In order for them maintain the upper hand. Which is how the two of them manage to maneuver around him. Until, George caught on to what they were doing. Which is why Louis killed him? According to Lisa's theory about what she thinks happened. Although, there seems to be a couple of snags along the way. Considering the establishment for which it connects Jill, Jason & Christian to the source. Linking them to the problem that contains to the murders. Which had Lisa wondering? What role does the three of them play in the killers game. Keep in mind? That there is a strong possibility that one of them holds the key to unlocking the mystery. That the answers she seeks lies within one of them. According to the killer's words.

Considering the fact that Lisa pick up a few pointers along the way. Which was taken from the video containing footage that maybe some use. Depending on how she labels certain aspects of the video. Like how Jason & Eric appear together that evening in the Galleria Hall? When there were already some speculations that Jason was the killer. Which added more fuel to the fire. Which is where things got interesting when Jason cross paths with Louis the alleged killer. Who happens to have on the exact same costume as him that night. Which brings up the assumption that by coincidence the two of them engage into an all out brawl. Which ended with Jason getting shot. Which is the tricky part about this whole incident the fact that Lisa couldn't tell whether Jason was involve in the scandal. However, there is that possibility that Jill could be the answer to the problem. Being that she is the only one out of the three that is constantly being harass by the killers. In which, Lisa can argue the fact that something doesn't set well with her. Containing to Jill history with the killers. That there is definitely something up with that issue? Which brings up the topic on Christian's involvement? The fact that he keeps looking over his shoulders. When something bad happens. A problem that sums up some interest on where he stands in all of this? It seems as if Lisa have some more digging to do. If she wants to uncover the truth behind this mystery.

However, Lisa decided to not share any of her information with the police. Do to the fact that she didn't want to alarm Jill & her two buddies about what is going on. So she decided to play it cool for now. Jill & Christian both were relieve that the nightmare is over. Even though, they still couldn't believe the ending results behind the shocking discovery. Jason however, was in disbelief about the whole thing. Considering how this all effects him emotionally about what just transpired? Of what was the purpose behind these murders? Which was the question on everyone's mind. That there were pieces still missing from the puzzle. That had Lisa wondering was it really over. The fact that all three of them were in total denial about the whole ordeal, but evidence provided by the police prove otherwise. According to the proof that has connect the two of them to the murders. Do to the evidence that was found in Eric's truck. That reveal multiple of costumes use in tonight's killings. Including the Faces of Death masks that has death written all over it's entire exterior. The concern on each one of their faces tells a story that somewhere's deep inside lies a dark secret. Which Lisa is determine to uncover the truth behind the mystery. Containing the past of Jill, Jason & Christian who's life still hang in the balance. That eventually the truth shall be expose to every news broadcast across the nation.